*"They're great kids," Eva said.
"And I've grown close to them, too."*

"I'm not surprised. You're a natural mother."

Her eyes brightened, and her cheeks flushed a pretty shade of pink. "Thank you so much for saying that. I've been worried about the kind of mom I'll be."

"You'll be the *best*. There's no doubt in my mind."

They stood just an arm's length from each other.

A wave of desire washed over Dan, and he was sorely tempted to reach out and touch her, to run his knuckles along her cheek.

Her lips parted—half in surprise and half in arousal. But she wasn't the only one whose thoughts had taken a sexual turn.

He wanted to kiss her again in the worst way. And in her eyes he could see that she wanted it, too.

Dear Reader,

It's summer in Brighton Valley, Texas, the fictional town where *His, Hers and...Theirs?* takes place. The sun is warm, and the days are lazy.

It's the perfect time for love, especially for a shy laboratory technologist who is pregnant—with twins!— and a rancher who has recently become the guardian to twins of his own.

I don't know about you, but I enjoy books with medical professionals and hospital settings almost as much as I do books with cowboys and ranches. So writing the BRIGHTON VALLEY MEDICAL CENTER series has allowed me to create stories with all my favorite elements.

So whether your summer reading takes you to the front porch, the seashore or a faraway place, I hope you enjoy Dan and Eva's romantic journey as much as I enjoyed writing it.

Happy reading!

Judy

P.S. If you want to know more about me and the books I write, please visit my Web site, www.JudyDuarte.com.

HIS, HERS AND...THEIRS?

JUDY DUARTE

SPECIAL EDITION

Published by Silhouette Books

America's Publisher of Contemporary Romance

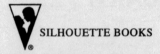 SILHOUETTE BOOKS

ISBN-13: 978-0-373-65543-4

Recycling programs
for this product may
not exist in your area.

HIS, HERS AND…THEIRS?

Visit Silhouette Books at www.eHarlequin.com

Printed in U.S.A.

Books by Judy Duarte

JUDY DUARTE

always knew there was a book inside her, but since English was her least favorite subject in school, she never considered herself a writer. An avid reader who enjoys a happy ending, Judy couldn't shake the dream of creating a book of her own.

Her dream became a reality in March of 2002, when Silhouette Special Edition released her first book, *Cowboy Courage.* Since then, she has published more than twenty novels.

Her stories have touched the hearts of readers around the world. And in July of 2005, Judy won the prestigious Readers' Choice Award for *The Rich Man's Son.*

Judy makes her home near the beach in Southern California. When she's not cooped up in her writing cave, she's spending time with her somewhat enormous but delightfully close family.

To Raema Pace, who not only gave me
a personal tour of the lab at our local hospital,
but also shares two grandchildren with me.

And to Emalee and Kaitlyn Colwell,
who have brightened our lives and hearts.

Chapter One

The playground at Twin Oaks Park was jam-packed with happy kids, and Dan Walker couldn't feel any more out of place than if he'd walked into a Sunday service at the Brighton Valley Community Church wearing nothing but his boots and his Stetson.

Of course, the family-style event was just what the pediatrician had ordered, and his five-year-old niece and nephew were having the time of their lives.

The grounds were hopping with mommies who wiped noses and kissed boo-boos and with daddies who played catch and flew kites. But it had been a real shot in the dark for him to think that he would somehow pick up everything he needed to know about fatherhood by attending a Parents of Multiples outing.

When Dr. Tomlinson had suggested Dan bring Kevin and Kaylee to play at the park, he'd been desperate and had thought he would give it a try. He figured it might be a good way to check things out without actually becoming a card-carrying member of the group. But being there had only made him feel less confident about doing right by the kids.

As his niece and nephew dashed around the playground, fitting right in with the sandbox crowd, Dan stood along the sidelines and watched. Too bad he hadn't decided to go the library instead. He could have checked out a copy of *Parenting For Dummies* or some other Daddy how-to book. Surely he would have picked up more information by reading than by osmosis at a family outing.

He supposed he ought to mosey on up to one of the real parents and ask, "How in the world do you do it? What's the trick?"

But he'd learned never to admit his shortcomings. In fact, if he ever thought he had a better than average chance of failing at something, he preferred to hit the high road rather than face the risk.

He chuffed at the irony, since here he was, the least capable adult in the bunch. But apparently Fate hadn't gotten that memo.

Last winter, on an icy Manhattan street, his sister, Jenny, who'd been struggling to make her mark on Broadway, had been struck by a car and killed.

When Dan had gotten the call, he'd been crushed. But it hadn't been the tragic loss of his twin sister that had torn him up. That had been tough enough. But what had made matters worse was that the two of them had been estranged for years, and her death meant they'd never be able to patch things up.

And then there were the kids. Jenny had been a single mom, and even though Dan had only been around Kaylee and Kevin once since they'd been born, there'd been a will, and his sister had named him their guardian.

The fact that she'd done that had been comforting in a sense. It meant that she hadn't completely shut him out of her life, that she'd known somewhere along the line that they'd eventually mend their rift.

Of course, who else was she supposed to leave them with? Their father had been a married man, which was one of several reasons Dan and Jenny had butted heads. So, he supposed, her options had been limited.

Either way, he wasn't sure what his sister had been thinking when she'd chosen him as the guardian of her children. After all, what in the hell did he know about being a parent?

At thirty-eight he was set in his ways, to say the least, and with some luck and a good deal of determination, he'd managed to avoid marriage and family himself. Of course, even though wedding bells and a wife were still out, apparently single parenthood wasn't.

After the funeral, he'd been prepared to take the kids back to the ranch with him in spite of all his insecurities. After all, he remembered how it felt to be young, homeless and unwanted. But it had been a stroke of luck for everyone involved when Catherine Loza, Jenny's roommate, had asked to keep the kids with her in New York for a while.

Dan had been uneasy about leaving them behind, but they'd been so comfortable in a big city environment, in the fourth-floor apartment where they'd lived most of their lives. Besides, they knew Catherine much better than they knew him. So all things considered, it had seemed like the best solution for the kids.

On top of that, Catherine was a woman, and Lord knew that all kids needed a mother figure. Dan sure would have liked having one when he'd been five.

So he'd left Kevin and Kaylee with Catherine, called them regularly and sent monthly checks to cover their living expenses.

But several months later, Catherine got a big part in a Broadway musical and called Dan in a panic. She was looking at a grueling practice schedule followed by evening performances that would keep her out late at night. She could no longer take care of the kids, and Dan had flown back to New York and brought them home to Texas.

And now, two weeks into the whole family ordeal, he hadn't gained much confidence, which didn't sit easy with a man who was proud of the fact that he could out-rope, out-ride and out-cowboy just about anyone in Texas.

But parenting two five-year-olds? That was a whole different ball game.

Dan adjusted his Stetson, making sure the brim blocked the sun from his eyes. Then he hooked his thumbs in the front pockets of his jeans and shifted his weight to one hip.

Damn, he wished he were anywhere but here today. But this wasn't about him; it was about the kids.

And right now, they were having a blast playing with the other twins and triplets, some of whom were dressed like mirror images of themselves.

But then again, why *wouldn't* Kaylee and Kevin be having a good time at the park? Living on a cattle ranch with the uncle they scarcely remembered and a crotchety old cowboy-turned-nanny couldn't possibly be any fun.

It was good to see them laughing and socializing, though.

Off to his right, he noticed a brunette who was also standing along the perimeter of the playground. She wore sunglasses, so he couldn't see her entire face, but her cover-girl profile and shape were intriguing.

She didn't appear to be a typical mom, although he couldn't put his finger on why he'd come to that conclusion. Maybe because her purse was way too small to fit in all the things some of the other mothers packed, like little baggies filled with snacks, wet wipes and Band-Aids. Or maybe because earlier this morning she'd somehow found the time to weave her long dark hair into a fancy braid that hung down her back.

She was dressed differently than the others, too, with a pink scarf that was stylishly wrapped around her neck, a crisply pressed white cotton blouse and a pair of slim-fit black jeans.

Whether she was a mom or not, he decided she was nice to look at—and that she was an intriguing diversion from the hubbub and the energetic chatter that swarmed around him.

Dan had been so caught up in his perusal of the brunette that he hadn't paid much attention to the activity on the playground—until a child let out a scream.

He watched the attractive woman dash across the sand toward the slide. As his gaze followed her, he realized that the screaming child was one of his.

Oh, God. His heart dropped to his gut, and his pulse kicked into overdrive as he hurried toward little Kaylee, who'd gotten hurt while Dan was supposed to be looking out for her.

The sight of blood running along the side of her face and her heart-wrenching screams shook him to the core.

Did he need any more proof of his shortcomings than that? He'd been gawking at an attractive woman, rather than watching the kids play, and he'd failed the kids, just as he'd known he would.

Hell, he wasn't cut out to be a father, no matter what Fate seemed to think.

He dropped to his knees on the sand beside them and started to reach out to Kaylee with stiff arms, but as the brunette continued to tend to the child, he pulled back his hands and let someone more capable do the comforting.

"Oh, sweetie," she said, lifting her sunglasses from her eyes and resting them atop her head. "What happened?"

"I...fell...down," Kaylee sobbed. "And I got hurt. *Really bad.*" She lifted her little hand to her forehead to probe the gash, and as she lowered it, she spotted the blood on her fingers and let out another wail.

"It's okay," the brunette said. "It's just a little blood. The owie isn't very big."

"Yes, it is," her brother said. "And it's bleeding a whole bunch. We better call the ambulance."

At her twin's suggestion, Kaylee cried even louder. Still, Dan thought a 911 call was probably their best bet. He knew that even the simplest head cuts could bleed profusely, but he'd much rather let a professional take charge.

The brunette made a quick scan of the playground and beyond. "Where's your mommy, honey?"

"She's in heaven," Kevin said. "She's watching over us, but I guess she was busy just now."

"I'm their uncle," Dan admitted. "This is Kaylee and Kevin."

The brunette turned to him. "I'm sorry. I didn't mean to interfere."

Her hazel eyes were almost amber in color, and her lashes were thick and dark, but he shook off the compulsion to study her. "Don't be sorry for stepping in. I'm way out of my league when it comes to this stuff."

"Do you have a handkerchief?" she asked.

"No, I never use them. Sorry." He realized one would have come in handy about now.

She smiled, then pulled the scarf from around her neck, revealing a nasty scar that ran from the underside of her chin down to her throat and beyond. A burn of some kind, he suspected.

She held the pink cloth against Kaylee's forehead, applying pressure to her wound.

"Are you a doctor?" Kevin asked the woman.

"No."

"A nurse?" the boy continued.

She slowly shook her head. "No, I'm not."

Then probably just a mother, Dan guessed. She'd certainly taken charge like a woman who'd done this a hundred times before.

"I do work at the Brighton Valley Medical Center," she told Kevin, "but not with patients. I'm a medical technologist."

"What's that?" the boy asked.

By this time, Kaylee seemed to realize that she was

under the care of a professional, and even if she didn't know what a technologist actually did, her scream had softened to a whine.

"I'm a scientist," the brunette said. "I work in the lab."

Whoa, Dan thought, realizing she was the brainy type. He'd never really known any of those. He tended to date women who were more street-smart than book-smart.

Dated? Now where had that wild-ass idea come from? If she was hanging out at the park with the Parents of Multiples, she was probably a mother—and married, which meant she was off-limits, even if he'd been looking. And he wasn't.

Still, his gaze slid to her left hand, which was ring-free. Not that it mattered, he supposed. His dating days were over now that the ranch house was filled with the pitter-patter of little feet.

Kaylee clung to the woman who dabbed at the wound with her scarf, permanently staining the fabric, no doubt. He'd have to buy her a new one when this was all said and done.

"Are you someone's mommy?" Kaylee asked.

"No," the woman said.

Then what was she doing at the park? Dan wondered. He almost asked but figured it might be best to bide his time and wait for one of the kids to quiz her. The two of them, especially Kevin, were certainly doing a pretty good job of interrogating her.

"Thanks for stepping in to help," Dan said. "Kaylee needed a woman's touch."

"You're welcome." Her smile reached her eyes, turning them to the shade of Tennessee bourbon. "Are you babysitting today?"

Was it *that* obvious he wasn't an experienced guardian? Probably, since a real father wouldn't have let one of his kids get hurt.

"I'm afraid I'm the man in charge," he said, faking a smile and doffing his hat. "My name's Dan Walker. And you're...?"

"Eva Galindo." She nodded toward the small building that housed the restrooms. "The bleeding has stopped, so maybe we should get some water and wash her face."

"Good idea." He stood, placed his hand on Kevin's head and stroked the straw-colored strands of his hair. "Come on, sport. We've got to get your sister cleaned up."

As they walked toward the restrooms, Dan said, "I really appreciate this, Eva."

"I didn't do anything out of the ordinary. I saw her trip in the sand and take a fall. I guess it was just instinct kicking in."

"Lucky me," he said, meaning it. Hopefully, Fate had decided to give him a break, at least for the rest of the day.

Eva took Kaylee into the ladies' room and came out several minutes later. The little girl's hair and face were wet but clean. And Dan was able to get a good look at the half-inch gash that marred the upper left side of her forehead and the bruise that surrounded it.

"What do you think?" Eva asked, gripping his gaze and setting his heart off kilter.

He didn't dare tell her that he was thinking of her as some kind of superhero right now. So instead, he glanced at her water-splattered, bloodstained white blouse and smiled. "I think I'm going to owe you a new outfit."

"That's not what I meant. Look at that gash, Dan. It's pretty deep."

The bleeding might have stopped, but the wound definitely gaped open.

"You know..." Eva cocked her head and studied the little girl's forehead. "She's probably going to need a few stitches."

"No!" Kaylee, who'd been a little standoffish with Dan the past couple of weeks, clung to the woman. "I don't want stitches."

If Dan had been looking in the mirror at his own face and had seen the cut, he would have let it pass without any treatment at all. But on a little girl?

"Why don't you want stitches?" he asked.

Kevin jumped in with the answer. "'Cause when we lived at our old house, Jimmy Milburn got stitches on his face and got to be a pirate for Halloween."

"Being a pirate is cool," Dan said, hoping to convince the kid that it was some kind of adventure, rather than something to be afraid of.

"Yeah," Kevin said, "but Kaylee doesn't like swords and stuff. She wants to be a princess. Besides, when I told Jimmy that I wanted to have stitches like his, he said it really hurt."

"It won't hurt Kaylee," Eva said. "She has a princess cut. And doctors are very careful when dealing with a princess."

The girl turned to Eva, her tears coming to a rolling stop. *"Really?"*

"Oh, yes. I'm sure of it." Eva ran her hand along

the dampened strands of Kaylee's long, blond hair. "The doctors at the medical center can spot a princess a mile away. And they know just what to do with royal injuries."

Kaylee cocked her head to the side. "They *do?*"

"Absolutely."

"Then, okay. I'll get princess stitches." Kaylee looked at Eva as though she were a fairy godmother.

But hell, Dan didn't blame the kid for that. He was thinking of Eva as though she'd fluttered into his life with a pair of wings and a magic wand, too. She'd been a real godsend, and he wished he could take her home with them until the kids turned eighteen.

"Will you ride with us to the medical center?" he asked her, hoping like heck that she would agree. Having her along would make the ordeal so much easier for Kaylee. And for him, too.

"Me? Well, I…" As her gaze caught his, he spotted more than indecision in her eyes. He noted apprehension, too.

Finally, at about the time he'd expected her to blow him off, she said, "All right, I'll go with you."

Dan didn't know when he'd heard sweeter words, when he'd felt more relief. "Thanks, Eva. I'll make it up to you."

Of course, he didn't have a clue how he was going to do that, but he'd figure out a way.

When Eva had set out this morning, she had thought the scope of her adventure would be simply checking out the Parents of Multiples picnic at the park and getting a feel for what would soon be in store for her.

Now, as she sat in the dual-wheeled Chevy pickup

across from cowboy Dan Walker, she felt as if she was living someone else's life. For a woman who was basically shy and introspective, it was both exciting and unnerving at the same time.

She wasn't one who basked in new experiences, and this was certainly a first for her. One minute she was on the edge of the playground, watching the kids chase after each other, and the next she was standing by helplessly while little Kaylee tripped and flew headfirst onto the steps of the slide.

Instinct had taken over, and Eva had rushed to the little girl's side. Looking back, she was thankful to know that her lousy childhood hadn't disabled whatever internal button had kicked in at just the right moment.

Thank goodness her instincts were functioning properly, since she'd be having a set of twins of her own in six months or so.

And now here she was.

She stole another glance across the pickup at the handsome cowboy in the driver's seat, wondering if she would have even given him the time of day on any other occasion. Not that he wasn't attractive, but he was well over six feet tall and as buff and brawny as the good Lord made them. He was just the kind of man who could easily toss stacks of hundred-pound bales of hay to the left and right without breaking a sweat. Yet there was something about the soft brown color of his hair and bluebonnet shade of his eyes that spoke of a gentle side.

That, she suspected, along with the way his expression had crumpled around the crying child, had made Eva trust him well enough to get into his truck in the first place.

Her stepfather had been a brute of a man who'd mentally—and sometimes even physically—abused her, so she tended to avoid men who reminded her of him. She'd had a couple of boyfriends in college—each of them budding scientists who had been brainy and slightly built—but the relationships had never lasted very long.

So when, after much thought, she'd decided to create a family of her own, she'd opted for in vitro fertilization. It had been easier that way. She hadn't needed to make any decisions about whether to have a man in her life or not.

She had to admit, though, that she was still a little apprehensive about being a mother and bringing home two newborns, which is why she'd come to the park today. She'd read about the Parents of Multiples event in the online newspaper and had decided to observe things from a distance.

It was a scientific approach to her problem, and it seemed to be the most logical way for her to proceed.

If she liked what she saw and the people she met at the park, she would take it a step further and attend one of the evening meetings, where she might connect with another mother of twins who could offer her advice— and maybe even friendship.

Of course, she hadn't been at the park long enough to observe much of anything when little Kaylee was injured.

She glanced over her shoulder and into the small backseat at the rear of the cab, where the twins sat in matching car seats.

When Kaylee's gaze met hers, the little girl smiled, but her bottom lip quivered a bit, as if she was trying to be brave. Eva's heart went out to her for the second time in just minutes.

According to Kevin, their mother was in heaven, which was sad. But there hadn't been any mention of their father or any indication of why the kids had come to live with their uncle. If Eva and Dan were alone, she might ask him, but she couldn't bring it up in front of the kids. Not when the answer might be painful for them.

As Dan pulled into the driveway that led to the Brighton Valley Medical Center and turned left toward the entrance of the E.R., Kaylee peered out the passenger window.

"Is this where the princesses come to get their owies fixed?" the girl asked.

"It sure is. And if we're lucky, my friend Dr. Nielson will be working. She's the royal physician, and she takes care of all the queens and princesses."

Kaylee settled back in her seat.

"You're good with kids," Dan said, sliding a grin her way. "I'm impressed."

His praise nearly knocked her off balance, since she didn't work with children in the lab. But she'd had to draw her share of blood when she'd been in training, and she'd learned a few tricks when working with frightened kids. Of course, once she'd graduated with her master's degree in biology, she no longer worked directly with patients.

"It's all in a day's work," she said, making light of what she'd just done.

"Then you deserve a raise," he concluded.

She had the strongest urge to look his way, but kept her eyes fixed on the road—or rather on the parking space he was pulling into. She still found it hard to believe that she'd agreed to ride with him. She certainly wouldn't have if his niece and nephew hadn't been with him.

But earlier on the playground, when Kaylee had thrown her arms around Eva and held on tight, the most stunning sense of warmth and wonder had flooded her chest. And so had a sense of awe.

Eva liked the way her emotional side had kicked in, which didn't happen all that often. But even more amazing was the realization that her own mother's abandonment and her stepfather's abusive nature hadn't damaged her in a way that might hamper her ability to love and nurture her own children.

At least, it didn't appear that way.

She reached up and fingered the side of her neck, where industrial-strength drain cleaner had splashed upon her skin, burning it all those years ago.

She kept the scar covered whenever she could by choosing turtlenecks and scarves to wear, but it wasn't the ugliness she tried to hide. She'd learned to deal with her flaws a long time ago. It was just that people— particularly children—would sometimes ask what had happened to her, and she didn't like to talk about it.

As an adolescent, she'd made up a wild story about an alien abduction, but who would believe a tale like that now? Certainly not the medical professionals with whom she worked.

Of course, she didn't usually mix or mingle with many of her coworkers outside the medical facility. And it was fairly easy to keep to herself while bent over a microscope in the lab.

The irony struck her as odd, though. For someone

who knew a lot of intimate details about people and their health, even before their doctors did, she kept her own secrets close to the vest. It was easier that way—and much safer.

"All right," Dan said, as he shut off the ignition. "We're here. Let's hope we won't have a long wait."

It was Saturday afternoon, and Eva suspected the E.R. would be packed, but that wasn't her main concern. She was more worried about what she'd say to Kaylee if Dr. Nielson, "the royal physician," wasn't working today and the little girl worried that she wasn't getting the proper medical care.

So while Eva climbed from the vehicle and waited for Dan and the kids to get out, she tried to come up with a plan B, but wasn't having much luck. After all, Betsy Nielson was great with children and would play along with the princess thing. Another doctor might, too, but Eva didn't know the others as well.

As they headed toward the E.R. entrance, a breeze blew across Eva's face and along her throat, causing the scar to tingle as if the years had rolled back and the wound was still in the healing stage, still pink and tender.

She knew it was just her imagination, but she turned up the collar of her blouse anyway, hoping to hide the scar, as well as the fear that she might not have healed completely—on the inside, where no one could see.

And that, in spite of how good she seemed to be doing with Kaylee this afternoon, that she might somehow fail her own children one day.

Chapter Two

Upon entering the E.R., Eva led the way to a triage area, where a nurse was posted to determine the priority in which the incoming patients would be seen.

Kaylee's condition certainly wasn't critical, and since the E.R. appeared to be especially busy today, Dan figured they wouldn't see a doctor until the cows came home. And if that were the case, he was going to owe Eva big-time for spending the afternoon at the medical center with them.

The triage nurse sent them to sign in with a clerk behind a desk who took Dan's insurance card. Thank goodness he'd put the kids on his plan after Jenny's death.

After providing all the pertinent information, he returned to the waiting area. There weren't many chairs from which to choose, so they opted for a grouping near a TV monitor that was set to the Discovery channel.

The kids and Eva zeroed in on the television, while Dan snatched a magazine from a table. He wasn't sure how long they'd had to wait before Kaylee's name was called, but he'd just reached the last pages of a battered, two-month-old issue of *Modern Horseman*.

As they all headed to the doorway that led to the exam rooms, the nurse who'd called them, a tall, slender woman with black spiky hair, looked at Kaylee and smiled. "What happened, sweetheart?"

"I fell down, and the slide hurt me."

"That's too bad. But don't you worry. We'll get you fixed up as good as new."

"Are you the princess doctor?" Kaylee asked.

The nurse furrowed her brow and cast a quizzical glance Eva's way.

"She's talking about Dr. Nielson," Eva explained. "Is she on duty today?"

The nurse smiled. "Actually, she *is* working. And we usually assign the children to her whenever we can. So your odds of seeing her are good."

Eva seemed to be relieved, although Dan wasn't sure why. Apparently that particular doctor was good with kids. Was she also a plastic surgeon?

The nurse—Shannon O'Reilly, according to her ID card—took Kaylee's temperature and checked her blood pressure, then she left them to wait for the doctor.

Kaylee nibbled at her bottom lip, and Eva eased closer. "Are you doing okay, honey?"

"I'm scared. I don't want it to hurt again. It's all better now, and I just want to go home."

Dan didn't know if she meant back to New York or the ranch, but he wouldn't ask. The kids didn't have any options about where they lived now.

Eva slipped an arm around Kaylee's shoulder, and the girl leaned into her. It was nice to see her connecting with someone. She'd been a little standoffish with him since he'd brought her to Texas.

He supposed he couldn't blame her for that. He didn't know squat about kids, especially girls. And he had a feeling she wasn't used to being around men, especially the rugged and outdoorsy type.

Moments later, an attractive redhead entered the room. She couldn't have been much more than an inch or two over five feet tall, but she had a definite, take-charge presence.

She introduced herself to Dan and Kaylee as Dr. Nielson, then greeted Eva. "Is this your family?"

"No," Eva said. "We're just…friends."

Dan would have corrected her if he could have figured out a better answer, but as it was, that would have to do.

As Dr. Nielson slipped on a pair of gloves, then examined the child's wound, Eva said, "Kaylee's a little concerned about getting stitches and looking like a pirate."

"Don't worry about that," the doctor said. "I've got something much better than stitches for this cut. We're going to use skin glue instead."

Dan eased closer, wondering if he'd heard her right. Was she really going to close Kaylee's wound with some kind of glue? Or was this all part of the magical princess-talk that Eva had been using on the child?

"Cool." Kevin eased closer to the exam table on which his sister sat. "Can I watch?"

"You certainly can." Dr. Nielson stepped aside, giving the boy a better view.

When the doctor was finished and Kaylee's wound was thoroughly cleaned, then sealed, Kevin stepped back and grinned. "It's too bad all the king's men and all the king's horses didn't have that stuff when Humpty Dumpty fell off the wall."

The doctor smiled at the boy. "You've got a point there. They might have been able to put him together again."

"So that's all there is to it?" Dan asked. "That bionic glue will hold together?"

"Yes, it will." Dr. Nielson removed her gloves and dropped them in the trash. "We can't use it on all wounds, but it should work out nicely for Kaylee."

"Just like magic," Dan said, realizing that it sounded as if he was slipping into the fantasy zone Eva had created. But that's not what he meant. He was thinking about the marvels of science and modern medicine.

The doctor reached for a clean rubber glove from the box and blew it into a balloon. Then she took a black marker and made eyes and a mouth near the base of the thumb, leaving the fingers to poke up like a Mohawk.

"Cool," Kevin said. "It has pokey hair like the nurse. Can I have one, too?"

"You bet." Dr. Nielson handed the blown-up glove to Kaylee, then reached into the box for another.

Dan looked over the sealed wound on his niece's forehead. He'd had plenty of stitches in his day—the gash in his knee for one—so he knew the routine for that. Kaylee would need an appointment for a checkup and suture removal. But what happened with skin glue?

"Does she need to come back?" he asked.

"Not unless you notice any unusual redness or

swelling." Dr. Nielson gave them some instructions about keeping the wound dry and protecting it. "In fact, after you check out at the discharge desk, you're good to go."

"Can I see my owie?" the girl asked.

Dr. Nielson found a mirror, then handed it to her.

As Kaylee peered at her reflection, she scrunched her face. "It still looks like an owie. You didn't do anything to make the cut go away."

"It takes time for it to get better," the doctor said. "The red line will turn pink before it disappears."

Kaylee didn't appear to be convinced.

"I think it looks like a fairy kiss," Eva said. "All good princesses have one, you know."

The little girl brightened. "Okay. And it's shiny because of all the fairy dust and magic."

If Dan was going to have to make up stories to appease Kaylee, she would be out of luck. His brain didn't work that way. He was more inclined to resort to one of the snide remarks Uncle Hank used to make when Dan had been a kid and had sprained a finger, scraped a knee or stubbed a toe. "Just go rub a little dirt on it and quit your whinin'."

But Dan couldn't say something like that to a little girl.

Besides, when he was twelve and had a cut along his thigh from a piece of barbed wire, Hank had used that line on him. He hadn't realized the old man hadn't intended for Dan to take him literally, and after following what he thought was sage advice from a real live cowboy, he'd gotten an infection along with a fever. He'd had his own medical emergency after that.

While Dan settled the account and signed the discharge paperwork, Kevin slipped up beside him. "When are we going to eat the picnic food?"

They'd had a late breakfast and hadn't been hungry when the other picnickers had spread out their lunches. So most of the food Dan had packed for them was still in a cooler in the back of the pickup. But he didn't feel like eating a bologna sandwich right now.

"I have a feeling that most of the people at the park have called it a day and headed home." Dan looked at Eva. "You've got to be hungry, too. How about going out to an early dinner with us? After that, I can take you back to your car."

The invitation seemed to take her aback, and before she answered she glanced down at her blouse, which was stained and crumpled.

"We'll go someplace casual," he added. "Maybe the Burger Barn or something."

"Oh, please!" Kaylee said to her new friend. "Come with us, Eva. I don't want to be the only girl."

At the child's request, the tension on Eva's face eased, and Dan was again struck by her natural beauty. By the delicate arch of her brows, by the thick dark lashes, by the intoxicating color of bourbon in those expressive eyes.

The collar of her blouse, which she'd turned up after removing her scarf, now drooped, revealing the scar she'd probably tried to cover.

"All right," she finally said. "And as luck would have it, I've got spare clothes in my locker at the lab. So if you don't mind giving me a few minutes to change, I'll go with you."

Kaylee let out a joyful little whoop, and Kevin appeared to be just as happy, which only went to show that kids were better off with a woman than a man. Of course, that wouldn't change the dynamics of the Walker household. They were stuck with two men.

"Do you want us to wait in the car?" Dan asked Eva.

"You don't have to. Why don't you come to the lab with me? You can see where I work."

"Sure," Dan said. He had to admit that he was curious about where the pretty scientist spent her days. Besides, he didn't have anything else planned for today, other than grabbing a bite to eat and then heading home.

So he and the kids followed Eva to the elevator and down one floor to the basement, where the lab was located.

Eva let them all in, then asked them to take a seat near the entrance while she changed clothes. "I'll just be a few minutes, and then I'll show you around."

Moments later, she returned wearing a cream-colored, lightweight turtleneck sweater and the same pair of jeans. She'd applied a touch of pink lipstick, and when she smiled, he noted a flush to her cheeks. He didn't think it had anything to do with makeup.

"Are you ready to check out the lab?" she asked.

The kids nodded and got to their feet. As Eva breezed past Dan, he caught the whiff of citrus—orange blossoms, maybe?

They followed her through the doorway and into a large room with white walls and various cubicles, where several people in white lab coats either studied machines or sat on stools and peered through microscopes. Eva said hello to her coworkers and introduced Dan and the kids.

"We're going to take a quick tour," she explained, as she moved through the lab.

Dan had never been behind the scenes in a hospital before and felt as though he was on some kind of field trip. Still, he found it interesting as she pointed out a refrigerator case that stored blood and blood products, as well as the several different machines and testing apparatus.

"So you're the one they call in when they need to take blood," Dan said.

"Actually," Eva explained, "the lab *technicians* are the ones who draw blood. I'm a *technologist* and work behind the scenes. I run the needed tests and send the results to the doctors so they can make the proper diagnosis and treat the patients." She led him to a cubicle that had a fancy microscope. "This is the station where I work."

"Who's that?" Kevin pointed to a photograph Eva had displayed on one of the sidewalls of her workspace.

Dan noted a smiling Eva, an elderly woman and a candle-laden birthday cake.

"That's Clara Morrison," Eva said. "She's a friend of mine. We were celebrating her seventy-sixth birthday that day."

"Wow," the boy said. "That's a lot of birthdays."

"It sure is." Eva reached into a drawer, pulled out a slide and slipped it into the microscope. "Here, let me show you what I do." She peered through the lens, then stepped aside to let the boy take a peek.

"Ooh," Kevin said. "I see a whole lot of little circles."

"I want to see them, too." Kaylee pressed against her brother. "Let me have a turn."

Kevin moved away reluctantly, then let his sister peer into the microscope. She'd barely had a chance to ooh and ah herself when he said, "Come on, Kaylee. It's my turn again."

Dan was tempted to ask for a turn himself, but he was too caught up in watching Eva move through the lab or in trying to catch another hint of orange blossoms each time she brushed past him.

As it was, he stood off to the side and remained an observer, a role he usually slipped into whenever he left the ranch. But not because he was shy or awkward. He just didn't open up around people he didn't know or trust.

Yet as he watched Eva blossom in her natural surroundings, her amber eyes brightening as she spoke to the kids, her tone soft and maternal, he couldn't help lowering his guard just a bit.

And looking forward to having dinner with her.

Dan figured the Burger Barn was their best choice for a meal, and the minute he stepped inside the family-style restaurant, he realized he'd been right. He placed their orders, then with Eva's help, carried their food and drinks on trays to the dining area.

"I'm not hungry anymore," Kevin said the minute he spied the colorful, indoor climbing structure that was designed to look like a big red barn with a yellow silo and blue netting.

"Not so fast, sport." Dan unloaded the drinks, burgers and fries onto the white Formica table. "You need to eat first, while everything is warm. You'll have plenty of time to play when you're done."

"Oh, okay," the boy said, plopping into one of the

white seats covered with a built-in blue vinyl cushion. He reached into his pocket and pulled out a couple of Matchbox race cars and a Star Wars action figure.

A few minutes later, both kids had wolfed down their kiddie meals and had finished their milk.

"See?" Dan said. "That wasn't so bad, was it?"

Without answering, the twins dashed off, leaving Dan and Eva to munch on their burgers and fries.

"Kaylee seems to be doing a lot better," Eva said.

Dan agreed. She'd been a real chatterbox at dinner, opening up for Eva more than she had for him in the past two weeks. And he had no choice but to attribute the change to the attractive woman seated across from him.

As he caught Eva's gaze, she leaned forward and lowered her voice. "So, where's their father?"

Before Dan could respond, Kevin slipped back to the table to pick up the little toys he'd left behind and said, "Our daddy's in New York."

Kaylee, who'd returned on her brother's heels, added, "He's rich and has a great big car."

"Yeah," her brother chimed in, "but we don't get to ride in it. He's too busy."

"He's *always* busy," Kaylee said. "That's why we never get to see him."

Eva glanced down at the half-eaten bag of fries resting in front of her, then back at the child. But she let the conversation drop.

When the kids took off again, she blew out a sigh, leaned forward and rested her forearms on the table. "I didn't mean to pry. Or to bring that up in front of them."

"I know. I thought they were out of hearing range, too."

"I take it their father isn't very involved in their lives."

"No, he isn't." Dan didn't want to go into all the details. When he'd found out his sister was dating a married man, he'd told her how disappointed he'd been in her. She'd tried to explain that she hadn't known at first, that the guy had kept it from her. And that when she'd told him that she was pregnant, he'd finally confessed.

Dan had tried to talk her into moving back home, but she'd refused. He'd never understood her need to move away from Brighton Valley in the first place, never understood her dreams.

After that, she'd been pretty tight-lipped about the kids and her personal life. But he'd never been one to keep quiet and had continued to let her know that he believed children should be raised in a loving, two-parent home. And that maybe they should be raised closer to family. But there was no need to go into any of that with Eva.

"Their dad has never really been a part of their lives," Dan said instead.

"That's too bad. They're cute kids."

"It's their old man's loss, I guess." He'd tried to tell himself that they were probably better off without him, which is what Jenny had insisted.

And maybe she'd been right.

All Dan really knew about Daddy Warbucks was that he was some Broadway bigwig who'd paid only a token amount of child support. And that Jenny hadn't wanted to make trouble for him by asking for more money. At least, that's what Catherine, her roommate, had said.

Dan opened a small bag of ketchup and squeezed a splotch onto his fries. He wasn't going to reveal more than he already had to Eva. It didn't seem fair to the twins—or to Jenny's memory. Still, he would have liked to have been able to say that his sister had known better than to get involved in a situation like that, but obviously she hadn't.

"I think kids ought to be raised by people who want them," he said.

"So do I. And I'm glad they have you."

Dan sure as hell wanted to do right by them. He'd feed them, clothe them and educate them by sending them off to college or trade school. But no one knew more than he did that kids needed love and affection, too, and he was afraid he'd fall short in that department.

"When did your sister die?" Eva asked.

"About six months ago."

"And you've had the kids all that time?"

"No, they just moved in with me a couple of weeks ago."

If Eva wondered why that was, she didn't ask. But for the damnedest reason, Dan felt compelled to explain. "After the funeral, my sister's roommate, Catherine, suggested that they stay with her. And it seemed like a good idea to me. They hardly knew me. I'd only seen them once—when they were three. My sister came for a visit, but she didn't stay long."

They'd argued, as they were prone to do, and she'd left earlier than she'd planned.

Eva remained silent, but seemed to be hanging on

his words. Her eyes asked, *And you agreed to leave them in New York with a stranger?*

"The only other option I had at the time was to take them away from their comfort zone and drag them back to Texas to live on the ranch with me, and, like I said, they didn't know me very well." He didn't mention Uncle Hank, who'd finished raising Dan and his sister, Jenny, when they'd had nowhere else to go. The crotchety old cowboy meant well, but he spent the bulk of his day grumbling about his lot in life.

"How are they doing?" Eva asked. "Was the move hard on them?"

"Probably. Who knows?" Dan lifted his chocolate milkshake and took a sip, relishing the cold, creamy drink. "Catherine recently landed her dream job—the lead dancer in a Broadway musical—and daycare became an issue for her."

To be honest, even if he didn't feel like sharing it with Eva, when he'd left the kids in New York after the funeral, he'd felt a little uneasy about the whole setup. He'd wondered how Catherine would handle the childcare on her own, but she'd seemed so sure of herself.

And, just as he'd suspected, when the kids had become too much for her to juggle, she'd contacted him and he'd immediately jumped on a plane.

"So now they're living in Texas with you," Eva said, connecting the dots with the information he'd given her.

"Yeah. That's about the size of it." If there was one thing to be said about Dan, it was that he tried his best to do the right thing, and that come hell or high water, he was loyal and responsible.

"What did you think of New York?" she asked.

"It wasn't my cup of tea." He preferred wide-open spaces and rolling hills to skyscrapers.

"How long were you there?"

"Too long." His flight had been delayed in Houston, and by the time he'd arrived in New York, it had been too late to get the kids. So he'd taken a cab to an over-priced hotel, where he'd been too keyed up to sleep a wink. Then he'd gone to Catherine's apartment the next morning and picked them up. "To be honest, I felt like a real fish out of water in Manhattan."

As awkward as he'd felt, as afraid as he was that he'd somehow mess up and do damage to their psyches and scar them for life, he hadn't been able to get them to the airport fast enough.

But once he'd brought the kids back to the ranch and tried to create some kind of family, he'd been more out of place than ever.

"How about you?" he asked.

"Me?" Eva reached for her milk.

"Have you ever been to New York?"

"I've always wanted to go. I'd love to see a Broadway show. But I doubt that I'll get to travel anytime soon."

"Why's that?" he asked, reaching for a fry.

"Because I'm pregnant."

His hand froze in midreach. "You gotta be kidding."

She wasn't, and he soon came to that conclusion.

"I'm sorry," he said, "but you don't look... pregnant."

"I'm only about three months along."

He paused for the longest time, the French fries long forgotten. "Is that why you were hanging out at the playground, watching the kids?"

"In a way. I'm not used to being around small children, so I'm intrigued by them."

"I never would have guessed that. You were so good with Kaylee. If you would have told me that you were a preschool teacher or a mother of three, I wouldn't have doubted it for a minute."

Eva couldn't help but smile. Her sole purpose for being at the park this morning was to learn how to parent and deal with two kids at one time, and here someone assumed she was a natural.

She certainly wouldn't admit otherwise. But it was nice to know that even after growing up in a dysfunctional family, she had what it took to be a loving mother and that she would have enough TLC to go around.

She lifted her apple juice and took a drink. "I didn't just chance upon the park today. I went specifically because I'd heard there was going to be an event sponsored by the Parents of Multiples. I was hoping to learn a few tricks in dealing with a set of twins."

He furrowed his brow, looking even more confused. "You have twins at home?"

"Not yet."

Before he could respond, little Kaylee ran to the table. "Uncle Dan, Kevin said you're going to give him a horse and teach him how to be a real live cowboy."

Dan nodded. "Yep, that's what I told him."

"But what about me? I want to ride a horse and be a real live cowboy."

"I thought you wanted to be a princess," Dan said.

The child nibbled on her bottom lip, then looked up at him with please-don't-say-no eyes. "Can I be both?"

Dan chuckled. "Sure. Why not?"

Kaylee broke into a bright-eyed grin. "And can Eva be a cowboy, too?"

"I doubt she'd like that," Dan said.

"Yes, she would." Kaylee turned to Eva, placing a small hand upon her knee. "You could ride a horse and everything."

Eva hadn't meant to encourage a relationship with the girl, though she could see how Kaylee had jumped to that conclusion. Now she needed to do some serious backpedaling. "I'll have to pass on becoming a cowboy, but maybe someday, after you learn how to ride, you can show me how it's done."

Kaylee quickly turned to her uncle. "Is it okay? Can Eva come to our house and watch me ride?"

"Sure," Dan said. "She can even invite her husband, if she wants to."

Apparently, he'd made the natural jump from "pregnant" to "married."

It seemed important that she set the record straight, so she said, "I don't have a husband."

"Sorry. I just assumed..." He shrugged. "Then bring your boyfriend."

"I don't have one of those, either."

Other than a twitch at the corner of his left eye and a slight crunch of the brow, he didn't respond.

She realized that he might have concluded that she'd had a one-night stand or an indiscriminate affair and, while it was none of his business, she felt compelled to explain. "I had in vitro fertilization."

Her decision made perfect sense to her. She would soon have her own little family without the involvement of another parent who might not look at things the way she did. But Dan's brow failed to completely relax until Kevin returned to the table.

A big grin was splashed across the boy's face. "See, Kaylee? I told you so. I'm going to be a cowboy, just like Hank and Uncle Dan."

"I get to be one, too," his twin sister countered. "And Eva gets to come to the ranch and watch me ride."

Kevin turned to Eva with a whopper of a grin. "Cool. You're going to really like it at the ranch. We got horses and cows and dogs."

"Mostly cows," Dan said. "It's a cattle ranch. And, of course, you're welcome to come out and visit anytime."

"Yeah," Kevin said. "Come home with us tonight and—"

"Whoa, there, pardner." Dan's voice held a dash of humor. "You can't just pick up people at the park and then ask them to come home with us."

"And as much as I'd like to see the ranch," Eva said, "tonight's not really a good time for me."

"Yeah, it'll be too dark." Kaylee turned to her uncle. "So how about tomorrow?"

Dan let out a little chuckle and turned up his hands in a what's-a-guy-to-do sort of way.

Eva thought for a moment as she felt her heartstrings being pulled by Kaylee and Kevin. She didn't have to go to work again until Monday, and she had no real plans for her day off.

She glanced at Dan and caught an intensity in his gaze that seemed to second the child's invitation.

"Okay," she said, surprising herself for agreeing so quickly.

Something told her there were a hundred reasons

she should steer clear of the little family, but as her heart strummed in the nicest way, she'd be darned if she could wrap her mind around any of them.

Chapter Three

Bright and early Sunday morning, Eva left her two-bedroom townhouse, climbed into her silver Toyota Celica and followed the directions Dan had given her last night. Then she drove about ten miles out of town.

As she continued along the county road, passing the landmarks he'd told her about—Sam Houston Elementary School, Roy's Feed and Grain and the Flying K Auto Parts Store—she realized she was getting close.

Cattle grazed in pastures along both sides of the road now, so she slowed, looking for the driveway that was marked by the big green mailbox he'd told her about, a plastic replica of a John Deere tractor. When she saw it, she turned left and followed the tree-lined driveway, her vehicle kicking up dust and gravel until she reached the house and outbuildings.

She parked by the barn, next to the pickup Dan had been driving yesterday, and shut off the ignition. She hoped she hadn't made a mistake by agreeing to visit the twins and their uncle, but she'd really enjoyed their time together last night, and getting to know the kids had been a special treat. Besides, spending time with them would be good practice.

Before she could open the driver's door, two cattle dogs ran up to her vehicle, barking to announce her arrival. Rather than get out immediately, she scanned the old clapboard house, noticing that the yellow walls and white trim had been freshly painted, that the shingled roof appeared to be new.

The front door swung open, and Kaylee stepped onto the porch. "She's here!" As the screen slammed behind her, she tore across the porch and down the steps with Kevin just a couple of strides behind her.

The dogs seemed to realize Eva was a welcome visitor, so she climbed from the car, shut the door and greeted the children. "Good morning."

"You came," Kaylee said. "You *really* came."

"I said that I would." Eva's gaze traveled back to the porch where Dan stood. She'd thought he was handsome yesterday, but he'd somehow morphed into a real live cowboy overnight, and she couldn't help but note the change.

He had an almost heroic aura now, as if he belonged on the set of a shoot-'em-up western.

Tall and lean, he hooked his thumbs in the front pockets of his worn denim jeans and moseyed toward her with a Texas swagger that made her breath catch.

"Did you have any trouble finding the place?" he asked.

"No, your directions were easy to follow." She tucked a strand of hair behind her ear, wondering if she should have braided it earlier. A pulled-back style would have been more practical for a day at the ranch, but as it was she'd fussed in front of the mirror long enough.

"Do you want to start with a tour?" he asked.

"Sure."

Something told her she ought to try and include the kids in the conversation, but she couldn't seem to tear her gaze away from the cowboy. That is, until the screen door squeaked, alerting her to the fact there was someone else at the ranch.

She turned to see an old man who appeared to be in his mid-seventies shuffle across the porch. He used a cane to support him, but his gait was a little unsteady. She'd assumed Dan and the kids lived here alone, although she didn't know why. They hadn't actually addressed the issue.

The old man carefully climbed down the steps. Upon his approach, Dan introduced him as Uncle Hank.

"Eva works at the Brighton Valley Medical Center," Dan added. "The kids and I met her at the park yesterday."

"You a nurse?" the old man asked.

"No, I'm a medical technologist."

"Sounds important."

Eva smiled. She liked to think her job and her contribution to the hospital were more than important; they were critical.

"Do you know Oliver Westfield?" Hank asked. "He's a dermatologist at the clinic."

"We've met," Eva said. "But I believe Dr. Westfield is a specialist in internal medicine, not dermatology."

"What the hell difference does it make?" the old man asked. "Far as I'm concerned, those doctors all *skin* ya." Then he chuckled to himself, pleased with his own humor.

"Actually," Dan said, "Hank likes Dr. Westfield, even if it sounds as though he's complaining."

"Liking him has nothing to do with griping about the bills he's been giving me." Hank leaned against his cane. "There was a time I could have given Doc Graham a couple of chickens and called it good. But now these young doctors want you to give 'em an arm and a leg, even when the ones you got ain't all that good anymore."

"Maybe you should see the princess doctor," Kaylee said. "She fixed my owie and didn't make us give her anything."

"So there you go," Dan said to his uncle. "You need a new doctor."

Hank chuffed. "I need a whole new body. This one's falling apart." He looked at Dan, challenging the man whose body was young and strong to disagree.

"You heard what Dr. Westfield said, Hank. All that whooping it up when you were younger is taking its toll on you now."

"I suppose that's true. Too bad I didn't listen to my Mama. She told me to quit smokin' and drinkin', but I didn't listen to her." He gave Kevin a little nudge. "Let that be a lesson to you, boy. Pay attention to what your elders tell you."

Dan placed a hand on his uncle's frail and stooped shoulder, giving it a gentle squeeze. "You want to take a tour of the ranch with us, Hank?"

"No. You go ahead. I'll have lunch ready for you

when you get back." Then the old man gave a respectful nod to Eva. "Nice to meet you, ma'am."

She smiled. "Same here."

Hank turned and shuffled back to the house.

"Come on," Dan said to Eva, "we'll start by showing you the barn."

The kids ran ahead, followed by the cattle dogs, and Eva fell into step beside her host.

"Hank's a good man," Dan said. "He's just a little old and crotchety. But he means well."

"You don't need to explain. I have a soft spot for the elderly. In fact, I've been volunteering my time at the Brighton Valley Senior Center."

"You don't say." He sketched a gaze over her, sending her senses reeling and knocking her off balance.

She did her best to shake off the inappropriate reaction to the look he tossed her way, telling herself there hadn't been anything to it, that her admission had merely surprised him.

But she hadn't done anything special. On a whim, she'd gotten involved with the center, hoping to fill and brighten the days and evenings when she wasn't working at the lab.

The game plan had worked, and as an unexpected bonus, she'd acquired a better understanding of those who were lonelier than she was.

"I wish I could tell you that Hank didn't always used to be cranky and ornery, but it wouldn't be true. He's been short-tempered and snappy for as long as I can remember. But for what it's worth—deep inside—he's a good man. And loyal to a tee."

"Buena jente," she said.

"Excuse me?"

"It's a Spanish term for 'good people.' You know, one of the white hats."

"Then that suits Hank just fine. You'll never find a man whose word holds more truth and follow-through."

Eva's steps slowed. "It must be frustrating for him to not be able to do the things he once could do with ease."

"I'm sure you're right. Hank used to be the king of the ranch, and now he sits in a rocker and guards the front porch. And instead of riding herd or breaking horses, he's babysitting Kaylee and Kevin."

"Is he good with them?" she asked.

"They're getting used to him."

What did that mean?

When they reached the barn door where Kevin and Kaylee had been waiting, Dan pulled it open and waited for them to all go inside. Then the tour began in earnest.

The twins introduced Eva to a pregnant broodmare named Sugar. Then, as Dan began to lead them back outside, Kevin said, "Don't forget about Midnight. She catches all the mice and rats that like to eat the hay and grain."

"Where is she?" Eva asked.

"Either napping or working," Dan said. "Midnight is a great mouser and a real asset on the ranch."

Once outside again, Dan showed Eva a few things around the immediate yard, like the corral where he kept a couple of cutting horses. Then they piled into the pickup and drove along a dirt road, where he pointed out the creek that ran through the property.

When he showed her a small, private lake surrounded

by cottonwood trees, she decided it was a beautiful stretch of land and told him so. What she didn't admit was that she was glad that she'd accepted the kids' invitation to visit. She couldn't remember having such an enjoyable day.

Kevin and Kaylee had both warmed up to her, and she'd felt a part of something for the first time in her life.

Okay, so she was an important member of the Brighton Valley Medical Center team, but she'd earned her spot by hard work and attention to detail. This was different. She'd been temporarily drawn into a family situation, and she hadn't done anything out of the ordinary to be completely accepted.

When they returned to the house, Dan parked near the barn. Eva wasn't sure how long they'd been gone—an hour or so, she suspected.

"Thanks for giving me a tour," she said. "I had a good time, and I'm glad I came." It had certainly been a lot better than hanging out at home, watching television or reading a book.

"You're welcome," Dan said, "but don't take off yet. Hank probably has lunch ready for us, although I hope you like bologna sandwiches. It's his specialty."

"Oh, not again," Kaylee groaned. "How come he doesn't like peanut butter and jelly? Or grilled cheese?"

"'Cause he's a cowboy," Kevin explained. "And that's what real ones eat."

"Then I'm going to be a princess instead. At least I'll get better food."

Once inside the house, Dan led Eva to the kitchen,

which was cleaner than she'd expected it to be with two men and a couple of kids living here.

"You sure keep things tidy," she said.

"We try. But to be honest, I have a woman who comes in every two weeks to clean, and she was just here yesterday."

"Can she help you with the kids?"

"No. She's got an outside job. When she comes here, she looks after them. But for the most part, it's just Hank and me."

Apparently the situation worked for them, but it was too bad they couldn't get a full-time nanny to come in and help more often. Hank didn't appear to be all that sweet and loving, and it seemed to her that the kids were missing a woman's touch. Not that Eva was of the mindset that men weren't able to nurture children. But Kevin and Kaylee had lost their mother recently, and with the way they both had seemed to draw close to her, she suspected there was some kind of maternal hole in their lives that hadn't yet been filled. And for that reason alone, her heart went out to them.

"I wish there was someone we could hire to come in more often," Dan said, "but I'll be darned if I know where to look. I'm under the impression that a bad sitter is worse than no sitter."

"I'm sure you're right about that. Maybe you should advertise and request references."

He shrugged. "That might work."

She was just about to tell him that she was sure it would, when an idea struck.

She'd really enjoyed her time with Dan and the kids. And last night, as well as earlier today, she'd found herself wondering if her life would soon be filled with similar days, with happy chatter and heartwarming smiles.

"Would you like me to help out for a while?" she asked.

"With daycare?" His brow furrowed into a V, and she could tell he'd been taken aback by the offer.

"I guess that's what I'm offering. I can come out to the ranch on my days off. At least until you find someone to take the job permanently."

The tension on his face eased some. "I hate to put you out."

"Well, it'll actually give me an opportunity to polish my mothering skills. And if you'd like me to, I can help you interview nannies. I'll need to hire my own daycare provider one of these days, so the research and the hiring experience will be eye-opening."

He seemed to struggle with the decision, and for a moment, she was sorry she'd offered.

"I hate to take advantage of your kindness," he said, "but to be honest, I could use someone in my corner."

"Then it's a deal." She reached out her hand in a playful but businesslike fashion, but when they touched, when their hands clasped, an unexpected thrill shuddered through her, and her heart skipped a beat.

She could have pulled away, could have ended the connection, but she'd never felt the like before. And for some reason, she wanted to relish the rush for as long as she could.

Eva returned to the ranch the following Saturday morning, but she didn't go empty-handed. From what she'd been told, Kaylee and Kevin were tired of bologna, which she assumed meant there hadn't been much variety to their meals. So she planned to make them a nice dinner tonight.

They probably had a few staples she could use, like flour, sugar and salt, but she doubted they'd have everything she would need. So after gathering a few items she had in her fridge and cupboards, she packed a box and carried it out to her car. Next she climbed behind the wheel, backed out of her driveway and headed for the ranch.

She wasn't sure what she'd do with the kids once she got there, but she'd think of something. Her few, precious childhood memories were of the time she spent in her *abuelita's* kitchen, where they made homemade tortillas.

As she left Brighton Valley city limits, an idea came to mind. Maybe she ought to make cookies with the kids. Assuming that Dan wouldn't be prepared with vanilla or brown sugar, she stopped at a little mom-and-pop market along the way. On the back of a package of chocolate chips, she found a cookie recipe, and she was set.

It was late in the morning when she finally arrived at Dan's place. One of the Queensland Heelers, although she wasn't sure which one, seemed to recognize her as a friend rather than a foe on this visit, hardly barking at all.

"Hey, doggie," she said, as she got out of the car. "Remember me?"

It certainly seemed to.

She hadn't taken two steps when the kids rushed out of the house, greeting her with happy smiles and chatter.

About that time, Dan stepped onto the porch wearing

a blue plaid shirt with the sleeves rolled up, revealing the muscular forearms of a man who worked the land. He also had on a pair of worn denim jeans and scuffed boots—nothing fancy—but he was certainly a sight for sore eyes.

Ever since heading home last Sunday afternoon, she'd had repeated visions of the man—and she wasn't always dreaming when he came to mind. But today, in the flesh, she found him more attractive than ever.

"Here," he said, closing the distance between them. "Let me take your bag."

"I'm afraid I've got more than just this to haul in." She clicked the remote on her key ring and popped open the trunk, which was full of groceries.

"You didn't need to bring food," he said. "I've got plenty. And what we don't have, I'll buy."

"I know, but I wasn't sure what you had in your pantry. And since I'm determined to make dinner tonight, I wanted to make sure I had all the ingredients. I hope you like Mexican food."

He brightened like a kid who'd been offered an early birthday present. "I love it."

As he reached into the trunk to lift the box, she noticed the edge of a bandage on his forearm.

"What happened?" she asked, pointing to the gauze.

"This?" He glanced down at his arm, then shrugged it off. "I got snagged by a nail in the barn. It's no big deal."

"Are you sure?" It must have been bad enough to warrant first aid.

He gave her a don't-worry-about-it grin, then lifted the box of groceries and closed her trunk.

Eva grabbed her purse from the front passenger seat of the car, pushed the lock button on the remote, then followed him to the porch, where two potted geraniums flanked the steps.

The wood slats creaked all the way to the front door, and they entered the house with the kids on their heels.

"I appreciate your help," Dan said, "especially today. I've got a lot of work to do and can't spare Manuel to help me. He's got to stick close to the barn this morning."

"Yeah," Kevin said. "That's because Sugar is going to have a baby, just like Jill."

"Not *just like* Jill," his sister corrected. "Sugar's baby is going to be a horse, and Jill had puppies."

Kevin nodded. "We'll take you to see them. Come on."

"Just a minute," Eva said. "I need to put away the perishable items in the fridge first."

"What's that?" Kevin asked.

Before she could explain to the kids, Dan excused himself and headed through the service porch and out the back door.

Eva couldn't help but watch him go, with that long, lean cowboy swagger of his. Nor could she help missing his presence. He might think she was a pro at dealing with children, but she knew better.

"Can I help you cook lunch?" Kaylee asked.

"Me, too?" Kevin chimed in.

Back to work, she thought, tearing her gaze away from the handsome cowboy and offering the children a smile. "Sure, you can help."

Kaylee pulled a chair from the table and dragged it to the counter. "What are we going to do first?"

"I'll tell you what," Eva said. "As soon as I get the beans going, we can make chocolate chip cookies for dessert. How would you like that?"

Kevin let out a little whoop for joy, and Kaylee seconded his opinion with a clap of her hands.

After she'd settled into the kitchen, Eva opened the pantry to see if the men did, indeed, have the staples she'd need—and they *didn't*.

How did they get by without flour or baking soda?

"We have a little problem," she said. "I brought chocolate chips, brown sugar and butter from home. But it doesn't look like your uncle has any flour. So we'll need to go the market. I saw one on my way here, so it shouldn't take us long."

Of course, she realized, as she peered into the refrigerator and saw how bare it was, she'd have to pick up things for lunch, too. She'd packed everything she needed to make a Mexican meal for dinner, thinking she would just make do with whatever Dan had on hand for the noon meal.

But after taking a quick inventory of the kitchen, she came to a clear-cut conclusion that rustling up a kid-friendly meal in the Walker house wasn't going to be all that easy.

Apparently, she was going to be limited to tuna, Vienna sausage or Spam. She suspected that if someone hid the can opener, the men would be at a complete loss.

"What are you going to make?" Kaylee asked. "We don't have peanut butter. Uncle Dan said he would buy some the next time he went to the store, but he didn't go yet."

"Then I'll have to ask your uncle what else he needs. I can handle the shopping for him. And if it's okay with him, I'll take you with me."

"Cool." Kevin eased closer to Eva. "Can we get Rocket-O's for breakfast? It's the kind of cereal that all the astronauts eat."

"We'll have to make a list," she said. "Do you know where your uncle keeps the paper and pens?"

"By the telephone. I'll go get some for you." Kaylee dashed out of the room before Eva could thank her.

"We're all out of candy, too," Kevin offered. "And chips. And Gummy Bears..."

"I was thinking about things like fresh fruit and veggies, almonds and raisins."

He scrunched his face, and something told her the shopping trip was going to be a brand-new experience for her. If truth be told, she might want to purchase healthy foods for them, but she was afraid she would be a pushover when the kids started pleading.

Ten minutes later, with her list in hand, Eva decided to let someone know what she was up to. She hadn't seen Dan since he took off earlier, so that left Hank. She found him in the living room, watching an old movie on television—a John Wayne western of some kind.

"I'm sorry to bother you," she said, "but the kids and I are going to the market. Is there anything you'd like me to pick up for you?"

"We're a little low on bologna," he said. "And I'm not sure what you got planned for dinner. I was thinking about Spam and eggs."

"I have everything I need to make tacos this evening, if that's okay with you."

The old man lit up. "Sounds great to me. I haven't had any Mexican food since Manuel's daughter came to visit last November."

"I can't promise that mine will be as good as hers," Eva admitted, "but I'll do my best."

"Don't worry about that. We aren't that fussy around here. I never could cook a lick, so ever since my Millie passed, we've had to make due with whatever I could come up with."

That explained it. Hank hadn't been a finicky eater who thrived on processed foods. He'd just been limited to whatever he could warm up on the stove.

"Are you sure there isn't anything else you'd like?"

"How about ice cream for dessert?" His eyes lit up, accompanied by a boyish grin that seemed to shave a couple decades from his face.

Eva smiled. "Sounds good to me."

Hank pressed his gnarled hands on the armrests of the chair and began to push himself to a stand. "I'll get my wallet."

"Oh, no. Please don't bother doing that. I've got it this time."

"You sure?"

"Absolutely."

"Do you know where I can find Dan?" she asked. "I'd like to let him know the kids and I are taking off for a little while."

"You might check in the barn."

"Cool!" Kevin said. "You can see the puppies, too."

Eva felt a rush of excitement, but it wasn't newborn puppies causing her heart to trill. It was seeing the handsome cowboy in his element.

Chapter Four

Dan hadn't been able to escape the kitchen fast enough.

Sure, he'd been eager to leave the kids in Eva's capable hands. That's why he'd hung around the house, waiting for her to arrive. Now that she was here, he was hoping to get some work done before the sun went down. It was already nearing noon, and he was as busy as a one-armed paperhanger. But there'd been another reason to duck out of the house.

He'd hoped to shake the unexpected surge of attraction that had struck every time he'd laid eyes on her. And if that weren't enough, he was still dealing with the heart-thumping effects, something he'd better kick—and quickly. So the old adage, "out of sight, out of mind," seemed like a logical game plan from here on out.

Besides, he had to talk to Manuel, the hired hand

who'd worked at the Rocking H for as long as anyone could remember. So Dan had pulled his hat from the rack near the service porch door and headed for the barn, where he expected to find the man.

Trouble was, the twins would be dragging Eva to the barn to see the puppies soon, so he'd make it a short conversation and take off before that happened. His business with Manuel wouldn't take long.

They'd been expecting a load of alfalfa for the past couple of days, and so far it hadn't shown up yet. He'd placed a call to Red Draper, the broker who'd promised it on Thursday, only to be told it would arrive this morning. But as far as he knew, it still wasn't here.

Red had given several explanations over the past couple of days. The first had revolved around a foul-up at the dispatch office. Then the truck had broken down. But the daily excuses were getting old.

As he entered the barn, he sought out the old cowboy and found him right where he expected him to be, near the stall that housed the pregnant mare with topnotch bloodlines.

When Manuel heard Dan's approach, he turned and leaned against the stall. "I think we're going to have a foal sometime today."

"Oh, yeah?"

Manuel nodded. "I sure hope things go better this time around."

So did Dan. The mare had lost her last foal, and they were hoping for the best this time.

Dan stroked the mare's neck, then asked, "Did that alfalfa ever show up?"

"The old hay-shaker who's supposed to unload it just got here, but so far, there's no truck yet."

Dan glanced at his wristwatch and shook his head. "I hope the damn thing didn't break down again. We're getting low. And I think we're going to have start looking for another broker, one who's more dependable. Yesterday when I was at the hardware store, I overheard some talk. It seems that Red might be in financial trouble."

"I hope he's not playing games."

That had been Dan's thought. He'd already paid for the hay he was supposed to receive.

The hinges on the barn door squeaked, and Dan looked up to see Eva enter with the kids. She glanced at him, and as their gazes met and locked, a surge of heat rushed through him, this one stronger than the last.

What was with that? Even if he was up for a little flirtation with the temporary nanny, he couldn't let things get out of hand. So he tossed her a generic, how's-it-going grin.

Her pretty smile just about lit up the barn, and he slowly shook his head, trying to get his mind back on his work.

Manuel didn't appear to be anywhere near as concerned about the hay as Dan was. Instead, he nodded toward the woman and kids. "What'd you go and do? Hire a babysitter?"

"Not exactly. That's Eva Galindo. And she's not a sitter. She's just going to help us out with the kids for a while."

"Good choice." A smile stretched across the old cowboy's craggy face. Manuel might be nearing seventy, but he still had an eye and an appreciation for an attractive woman. "Lucky you."

"The kids are the lucky ones. She's a lot better at

dealing with them than I am. And before you get any funny ideas, let's get something straight. Eva's just a temporary fix. She's agreed to help out once in a while until I can hire someone permanent."

"If I were you, I'd be dragging my feet when it came to putting out any ads in the employment section of the paper." The older man's grin shifted and his eyes sparked with humor. "Eva looks like a keeper to me."

"Yeah, well, that's not an option. She already has a job—a good one down at the medical center. So I'm lucky that she's willing to help out on the days she doesn't have to work until I can find someone to hire permanently."

Still, he couldn't help but steal another glance her way, just as she and the kids knelt beside the mother dog and her litter. He watched Eva lift one of the newborn pups and hold it to her cheek.

Dan turned away from the sight, struggling not to stare, just as Kevin called out to him. "Uncle Dan, when we're done looking at the puppies, can me and Kaylee show Eva the rope swing you made when you were a boy?"

"If she'd like to see it. But I don't want you using it until I get a chance to test the knot. It's been hanging there for a long time, and I need to make sure it's secure."

"Where is it?" Eva asked as she got to her feet and brushed the straw and dust from her jeans.

"It's in an old oak tree about two hundred yards to the east."

"I can show you," Kevin said. "It's not very far away. When Uncle Dan first came to live here, him and his friend made a fort and a swing."

The friend had been Luis Mendez, Manuel's nephew. Luis had spent his summers on the ranch, and the boys had become close over the years. But while he was living at home with his mom during his senior year in high school, he'd been involved in a car accident and had been seriously injured.

Luis should have lived, but there'd been complications during surgery, and...well, he hadn't, and Dan had taken it hard.

The fort had been a painful reminder of how rough, how empty, how hollow Dan's life had become without a friend to confide in. So one day, while he'd been feeling sorry for himself, he'd torn it down. But the swing remained.

"Do you want to come with us?" Eva asked.

He slowly shook his head. "No, you go on. I've got a ton of work to do."

As Eva and the kids walked out of the barn, Dan felt an eerie sense of loss and disappointment.

And he'd be damned if he knew why.

After the kids had shown Eva the pups and taken her to see the old rope swing, she rounded them up and went looking for Dan to ask his permission to take them to the market.

She found him saddling one of the horses in the corral near the barn.

"If it's all right with you," she said, "I need to pick up a couple of ingredients I didn't think to bring. And I thought I'd take the kids with me."

"No problem." He finished cinching the leather strap on the saddle, then reached into his rear pocket for his wallet.

"I'll get it," she said. "You don't need to—"

"I insist." He handed her a twenty. "Is that enough?"

"Yes, unless there's something else you'd like me to pick up for you."

"I'm running out of razors." His gaze met hers, and for a moment they seemed to be caught up in the same vision—a steamy bathroom mirror, an after-five shadow, a towel-clad body.... But he seemed to shake it off faster than she could.

"On second thought," he said. "I'll pick that up my-self. I've got to run down to the feed store later this afternoon anyway."

"I don't mind...."

"Thanks. I appreciate the offer, but there are some things that are probably easier to do myself."

Then he'd led the horse out of the corral, locked the gate and mounted, the saddle creaking from his weight.

"Have fun," he told them as he tipped his hat and took off.

If Eva hadn't known better, she would have thought that he'd been in a hurry to get away. But she figured he was busy and had a lot of things to do.

After a quick trip to the market, where they picked up creamy peanut butter, grape jelly, flour and a gallon of vanilla ice cream, she and the kids were back in the kitchen.

Apparently, while she'd been gone, Hank had fixed a quick meal for the men—bologna, she suspected. He'd cleaned up after himself, but she could tell that he'd been at work. The loaf of bread was only half the size it had been when she'd first seen it in the pantry, and the jar of sun tea that had been brewing on the counter was empty.

It was just as well, she decided. She didn't need to worry about feeding anyone other than the kids. So she made peanut butter and jelly sandwiches, sliced apples and poured three glasses of milk, much to Kevin's delight.

"You sure are a good cooker," he said, as he munched.

Kaylee nodded in agreement, and Eva grinned, basking in their praise, even though she really hadn't done anything to earn it.

After lunch, she cleaned off the table, then laid out the ingredients for the cookies.

"This is going to be fun," Kaylee said.

Eva thought so, too. She could have made quick work out of mixing the dough, but she took it slow, waiting for the kids to measure and to stir the ingredients.

When the first batch came out of the oven, even Eva was hard-pressed not to eat her fill; she loved chocolate. But they stacked most of the cookies on a plate to serve with the ice cream at dinner.

"You sure are a good cooker," Kevin told her again.

"We're *all* good cookers," Kaylee corrected.

"That's right. I'm sure glad you helped me." Eva smiled at the kids, wondering what her twins would be like when they were five. Would one be outgoing and effervescent like Kevin? Would one be as introspective as Kaylee?

Either way, she was looking forward to motherhood, and being with the Walker twins would be good practice.

"So now what're we going to do?" Kevin asked. "Can we help you cook dinner?"

"I suppose so." Eva wasn't sure what they could do to help, though. There wasn't much to whipping up some Spanish rice. And the beans were already simmering on the stove. Chopping lettuce and tomatoes wasn't a safe chore for small children. And grating the cheese might not be much better.

"How would you like to help set the table?" she asked.

Kevin grimaced. "What's fun about that?"

"Well," Eva said, putting on her thinking cap, "you could look for some flowers to put in a vase as a centerpiece. And maybe you could use your crayons to make little cards that would tell people where they're going to sit."

"I know where we can find flowers," Kaylee said. "In those pots by the front porch. Come on, Kevin."

The kids were off before Eva could blink.

That was the trick, she decided. She'd need to keep one step ahead of the kids at all times—and she'd have to be creative.

She finished cleaning up the mess they'd made while baking the cookies, then peered into the pot of beans that simmered on the stove. So far, so good.

Preparing a family dinner for the Walkers was going to be a real first for her, and she hoped she didn't screw it up. But she had an idea everything would work out okay in the long run.

She'd always been intrigued by recipes and decorating articles in magazines, so she at least had an intellectual handle on both cooking and entertaining—even if she'd never considered herself a homemaker by any stretch of the word.

Of course, she enjoyed throwing together a tasty meal at times, but it really wasn't much fun cooking for one so she rarely went to the extra effort.

Heavy boot steps sounded on the back steps, and when the door swung open, Dan entered the service porch carrying an empty plate and the jar that once held tea.

"I thought I'd better bring this back inside so we can brew more tea for dinner," he said. "Unless you have something else in mind."

"No, tea sounds good." She watched as he entered the kitchen and headed for the counter. He had a smudge of dirt over his left brow, which made him appear down-to-earth, hardworking and manly.

As he brushed past her, she caught a whiff of leather, musk and...cowboy.

In spite of herself, she found herself drawing in another slow, steady breath, trying to take in more of his rugged scent. And as she did, something stirred deep inside of her, something uniquely feminine.

"Is everything okay?" he asked, clearly zeroing in on her expression.

What had he seen in her eyes? Something giddy and girlish? Something a lot more womanly and heated?

Doing her best to shake it off, she managed a smile and said, "I'm good. It's fine."

"Can I get you anything?" he asked.

"No, I'm finding my way around the kitchen. Thanks."

He nodded, as if everything was fine, then

headed outside, leaving her to ponder what had just happened—at least, in her mind.

Before she could give it much thought, the screen door slammed in the front part of the house, drawing her from her musing.

"Hey!" Hank barked out from the living room. "What did I tell you kids about slamming the door. Take it easy."

"Sorry, Uncle Hank," Kevin said, his small footsteps suggesting he was still on the run.

"We forgot," his sister added.

As the kids entered the kitchen, Eva turned away from the stove to see them both holding a bouquet of geraniums.

Kevin thrust his at her. "We got the flowers, Eva. Will these work?"

"They're very pretty. I wonder if your uncle has a vase to put them in."

The kids looked at each other and shrugged.

"Well, I'll just have to look."

When she didn't find an actual vase, she took a small drinking glass from the cupboard and filled it with water. Then she handed it to Kaylee so she could add the flowers.

As soon as the glass was filled, Kevin took it from her. "I'll put them on the table."

"And I'll go get the crayons and the paper," Kaylee said, as she dashed out of the room.

Eva watched as Kevin pulled out a chair, climbed on it and carefully placed the centerpiece on the table. He moved it to the right, then back to the left.

When he was finally satisfied with the placement, he turned to her and grinned.

"Good job," she told him.

He beamed at the praise. "It's been a fun day. We got to make cookies and fix dinner. My mommy used to let me and Kaylee help her all the time. We really like having you here, Eva."

Talk about raising the bar...

She offered the child a halfhearted smile, hoping he didn't sense her apprehension. It was one thing trying to compete with another woman's cooking, but another altogether trying to live up to someone's mommy.

At a quarter to six, Eva set the table and filled the serving bowls with beans and rice. Next, she put out some grated cheese, chopped tomatoes and shredded lettuce, thinking everyone could stuff their own tacos.

As soon as she'd fried the last corn tortilla shell, she asked Kevin and Kaylee to call the men to the table. And while they were gone, she prepared plates for the kids, giving them small scoops of rice and beans.

When the twins returned with Hank, Kevin said that Dan was in the office and would be coming shortly.

"I told him I was pretty darn hungry, so he'd better hurry," Hank said with a grin. She was eager to have Dan join them, too.

A little too eager, she decided.

She tossed the older man a smile, then asked the kids if they wanted cheese, lettuce and tomatoes in their tacos. She assumed the salsa was out.

"Cheese is okay," Kevin said, "but I don't want any salad in mine."

"It's not salad when it's in tacos," Eva said. "Why

don't you give it a try? If you eat it all together, you'll be surprised at how good it tastes."

"He's a cowboy," Dan said, as he entered the kitchen. "And everyone knows that a cowboy will at least taste anything the hostess puts in front of him."

Dan glanced at Eva and shot her a conspiratorial grin that turned her heart on end, then returned his focus to Kevin.

The boy's mouth scrunched, but he pulled out his chair and took a seat at the table. "Okay, I'll try it."

Moments later, the men were soon making appreciative noises over the spicy taste of the homemade tacos.

Hank, whose forearms rested on the table, lifted his head and grinned. "I gotta tell ya, ma'am, this is the best Mexican dinner I've had in ages. You're one heck of a cook."

"Thank you. I'm glad you like it." Eva was both pleased and relieved that the tacos had gone over so well, but it was Dan's gaze she sought, his approval.

When he returned her smile, she relaxed long enough to reach for the bowl of rice and begin filling her own plate.

"I'm looking forward to a homemade Sunday dinner," Hank said. "I don't suppose you'd consider making pot roast? It's my favorite. Whenever I get an itch for some good cooking, I have to drive into Brighton Valley and eat at the café."

Eva had never tackled anything that huge before. Okay, so she'd taken on dinner tonight and had passed with flying colors, but she felt fairly competent at cooking Mexican food.

Trying to fix a meal that Hank's late wife had probably whipped up regularly—something he favored—wasn't the same thing. Maybe she ought to give Betsy Nielson a call and ask for a few pointers.

"Hey!" Kevin brightened, his mouth full, his jaws working. "You were right, Eva. I can't even taste the salad when it's inside the tacos."

"I'm glad to hear it." Satisfied that everyone was seated and served, she took her own place at the table and filled her plate.

Hank, who was munching away on his second taco, looked up from his nearly empty plate and said, "You're a wonder in the kitchen, Eva. I'll say it again—this is the best meal I've had in ages."

She ought to feel flattered, but the compliment was a little unsettling. She had no trouble dealing with praise in the laboratory. But here? When she was so completely out of her element? When she'd so badly wanted to impress them yet didn't know what to do as an encore?

Still, she couldn't very well make excuses or downplay the praise, so she smiled and thanked the elderly man.

They continued to eat, and when they'd all had their fill, Eva excused herself to bring out the dessert, the vanilla ice cream and homemade chocolate chip cookies that she and the kids had made earlier.

Hank's praise seemed to escalate with each bite he took. "I'll tell you, it don't get any better than this."

"He's right," Dan said. "The food is great, Eva. You're spoiling us."

Her heart strummed at the younger man's praise, and she watched him reach for seconds.

Everything about Dan Walker intrigued her—the way he held his fork, the way he studied his plate.

When his gaze lifted again, when his eyes met hers, something shot right through her, and her heart rate went haywire. She scurried to find a way to shift the focus away from him—and from anything romantic.

"The cookies make all the difference," Eva said. "And you have Kevin and Kaylee to thank for that."

"We like to cook and bake stuff," Kaylee said. "Me and Kevin can help Eva do it everyday."

"Yeah," her brother chimed in. "It's fun to make cookies—and it's even more fun to eat them. But after dinner we like to watch TV. Can we do that before we have to take our baths?"

As Dan gave the okay, Hank pushed back his chair. "I can't manage another bite, so I may as well turn on the television for them."

When Hank and the children left the room, Dan stood and began to clear the table.

"You don't have to do that," Eva said. "I can get those."

"I'd feel like a real jerk if I let you clean up after us, too. It's bad enough that you're here on your day off and that you slaved over the stove all afternoon."

"It wasn't a chore. *Really.*" In fact, she'd actually enjoyed making dinner and baking cookies with the kids. It gave her an opportunity to see how the other side lived. And so far, she liked what she'd seen.

She'd already wiped down all the countertops before they'd eaten, so it was just a matter of putting the leftovers in the refrigerator and doing the dishes.

"Why don't you wash," Dan suggested. "Then I'll dry and put them away."

"Sounds good to me."

She'd no more than filled the sink with warm, soapy water when the service porch door squeaked open and footsteps sounded on the linoleum flooring.

Eva glanced over her shoulder to see the ranch hand—Manuel—entering the kitchen.

Where had he been? What had he eaten? Maybe she should offer to feed him. In spite of how many tacos Dan and Hank had wolfed down, there was still plenty left to make another plate.

"Boss?" the old cowboy said. "I'm sorry for busting in on you—"

"What are you still doing here?" Dan asked. "I thought you and Sylvia had company coming to-night."

"Yep, we do. And I'm supposed to stop and get some butter on the way home. But I got caught up trying to make sense of that bill we got from Hennessey's Feed and Grain. Those blasted invoices weren't lining up with the statement." The old cowboy chuckled. "I'd probably still be working on them if Sylvia hadn't called to ask what was keeping me. So I set everything aside and took one last look at the mare before leaving."

Dan made a quick attempt to fold the dishtowel he'd been holding, as if knowing that whatever had sent Manuel to the house would take priority over the dishes. "So what's wrong?"

"Nothing. The mare dropped her foal."

"You're kidding!" Dan's movements froze. "When did that happen?"

"Just a few minutes ago. The filly's still wet." Manuel broke into a grin. "And you ought to see her. She's a pretty little thing, too."

Dan started to cross the kitchen, then stopped and turned back to Eva. "Her first foal was a stillborn, so we've been watching her pretty close. But apparently that wasn't necessary. Come on out to the barn with us, and you can see the newest addition to the ranch."

"I'd love to." She reached for the dishtowel he'd just discarded and dried her hands. Then she followed the men out to the barn.

"It's becoming a nursery in here," Manuel said, as he nodded to the corner where Jill nestled her pups in a bed of straw.

Eva glanced at the mama dog, then continued to the stall that housed the mare and her new filly—a black, spindly legged horse, with a white star on her forehead and a stubby little tail.

"Oh, look at her." Eva moved as close as the railing would allow. "Isn't she cute?"

"I guess you could say that," Dan said. "But the real value is in her bloodlines. Her mother is the best cutting horse any of us have ever seen."

They watched as the foal latched on to her mother's teat and began to nurse.

"Well, there's no point in me staying here," Manuel said. "I've got to get home before my wife thinks I'm avoiding her brother and his wife."

"I'll see you on Monday," Dan said.

"You bet."

As the ranch hand left, they continued to watch the mare and her filly for several more minutes. Then Eva decided she'd better go inside and finish the dishes. The kids would need their baths soon, and she couldn't lollygag outside, no matter how sweet the sight.

"I guess I'd better get back to work," she said.

"Okay," Dan said. "I'll be right behind you."

As Eva left the barn, she paused outside long enough to inhale the night air, which was laced with the scent of alfalfa and night-blooming jasmine. She caught the sound of crickets chirping, a horse nickering in the distance.

When the barn door squeaked closed, and the light dimmed, she turned to see Dan approach. In the shadows of night, he appeared larger and more impressive than ever, and she was reminded of Wyatt Earp walking along the streets of Dodge City, making sure all was well.

"What are you doing?" he asked.

"Nothing. Just taking in the sights and sounds of the ranch. I'm not really what you'd call a city girl, but this is all new to me."

"Do you like it?"

She nodded, and in the soft light from the house, she watched a smile stretch across his face.

"Do you feel up to taking a little after-dinner walk?" he asked.

The offer took her aback, yet in spite of knowing there were kids inside the house who needed baths, she found herself nodding. "Sure. If you're up to it."

"Why not?"

He shot her a grin that caused her heart to jump and make a swan dive into the pit of her tummy, then he nodded to his right in an after-you way.

The soles of his boots and her shoes crunched along the gravel as they walked, following a path that ran along the corral nearest the house.

"Dinner was great," he told her for the second time this evening. "Having you here is going to be a treat."

His compliment was touching, maybe even more than it should be. "Well, thanks for letting me get a little practice at raising children."

"I guess it's a win-win situation, although I can't help thinking that we're getting the best of it."

She pondered his comment for a moment, then decided not to address it. Instead, she said, "I think we ought to advertise for a nanny. It could take us a while to find someone loving and trustworthy. Would you like me to call the newspaper tomorrow?"

"Sure."

They walked side by side, their path lit by the floodlight that was perched at the side of the house. She had the strongest compulsion to slip her hand into his, but how brazenly wacky was that?

So to counteract the urge and the effect his presence was having on her, she tucked her hands into her pockets. She'd only taken a couple of steps when she reached a soft spot in the dirt. Her foot twisted, and her ankle wobbled.

She caught her breath, thinking she was going to take a tumble before she could get her hands out of her pockets to brace her fall, when Dan wrapped one arm around her and grabbed her wrist with the other.

"Are you okay?" He held her tight, steady, and his gaze sought hers.

The warmth of his grip, the strength of his support and the scent of leather and musk sent her senses reeling.

She straightened, yet he continued to hold her. And something surged between them, something magical that settled deep within her core. For one sweet moment, she thought he might kiss her—and hoped that he would. Her heart both soared and pounded, as though trying to take flight.

If she'd been a little bolder, she might have placed a hand on his cheek, drawn his lips to hers. But she'd always felt backward when it came to men, to dating, to…sex.

What if she was misreading something? What if she reached out, only to have him pull away?

She couldn't take the risk. She'd have to wait for him to make the first move.

Do it, she thought. *Kiss me.*

Please.

Her face tilted upward, and her lips parted, oh, so gently in an invitation—at least, that's how it seemed to work in the movies. Her breath stilled as she waited.

Then he let go, his hands dropping to his sides, and stepped back. "Are you sure you're all right?"

Physically, maybe. But she wasn't so sure about how she was doing emotionally.

"I'm fine," she lied, her voice wavering just a tad. She tossed him a smile to mask her embarrassment and confusion.

"Maybe we ought to head back to the house," he said. "The ground out here is softer than I'd thought, and I'd sure hate to see you fall."

She didn't want that to happen, either, although she was entertaining a different type of fall—the emotional kind. And she wasn't prepared for anything like that.

"You're probably right," she said, realizing a kiss would have complicated their lives.

Still, as they headed back to the house, she couldn't help but swallow an ache of disappointment.

Chapter Five

Thanks to stewing over the kiss he'd almost stolen from Eva last night, Dan had tossed and turned until after midnight.

What had he been thinking?

Thank goodness he'd pulled back and gotten things under control. Kissing the temporary nanny would have really sent his world topsy-turvy.

Some women—and he would bet the farm that Eva was one of them—took kisses seriously. God only knew how a pregnant woman would react to that kind of thing.

Hell, for a moment, he'd suspected that she'd wanted a kiss as much as he had, and then where would that have left him? Up a creek, most likely. And dodging a commitment of some kind.

No, a relationship with Eva was completely out of the question. So the first thing he had planned to do on

Sunday evening, once she was out of the house for good, was start searching for a housekeeper/babysitter.

He might not be able to find anyone better with the kids than Eva was, but that wasn't nearly as important as finding someone who didn't send his head spinning, his blood pumping and his hormones swirling. So he'd make sure he hired an old, frumpy and unattractive woman to handle childcare, some light housekeeping and a little cooking.

She'd be loving and kind to the kids, of course. But he didn't need to have his thoughts scattered and his life turned on edge.

However, that game plan didn't do anything about getting him through the day and into the evening.

He'd managed to be out when Eva arrived this morning, but he'd run out of things to keep him busy. Besides, he was getting hungry. But that was okay. At least he'd have Hank and the kids to keep the conversation going in a safe direction.

So he rode back to the house, dismounted and removed the saddle from the gelding.

"Uncle Dan?" Kevin called, as he crossed the yard to the corral.

"Yes?"

"Where have you been?"

"Out and about." He reached for the brush and began cooling down his mount. There was no need to give the kid any more explanation than that. He couldn't very well admit that he'd been killing time until he could return home without having to risk being in close quarters with Eva any longer than necessary.

"That's too bad," the boy said. "You missed out on all the fun."

"Is that right?" Dan glanced at his nephew, glad the day had gone well.

"Yep. Eva brought coloring books and markers today. And me and Kaylee got to make stuff. We also played a cool card game."

"I'm glad to hear it."

"You should have been here."

Nope. It had been better that he'd stayed away. Out of sight, out of mind.

Trouble was, she'd remained in his thoughts anyway.

"Oh!" Kevin said, as he climbed up the wooden rails of the corral. "I almost forgot to tell you. Eva said that dinner's ready."

"Good. I'm hungry." And besides being eager to eat, the sooner Dan could thank Eva for her help and insist upon doing the dishes tonight so she could go home, the better off they'd all be.

"And do you know what?" the boy added. "The food smells really good."

Dan was sure that it did. He could almost imagine the succulent aroma of sizzling pot roast juices now. "Tell her that I'll be there in a minute."

He wondered if she'd made dessert again. If not, he suspected they still had some ice cream left in the freezer.

As Kevin continued to play on the fence, Dan turned the horse loose and carried the gear into the barn. He'd no more than hung up the saddle and bridle when a thump sounded outside.

What was that?

He didn't hear a cry, but something didn't seem right. And while he had no explanation for his immediate reaction, he rushed out of the barn, only to find Kevin sprawled on the ground, trying to catch his breath. His eyes grew wide, as he opened his mouth. But no words came out.

"It's okay," Dan told him, as he knelt beside him. "You just knocked the wind out of yourself. Relax, and you'll be okay in a minute or so."

Finally, the boy gasped, then cried.

There was a scrape on his chin, and a dribble of blood on his lips. Dan didn't think it was serious. Still, he picked him up and carried him to the house—to Eva. A kid needed a woman at a time like this.

And he'd been right to go to Eva.

Just as if she had eyes in the back of her head or sensed them coming—hell, maybe she'd just heard the kid crying—she opened the back door and stepped aside so he could carry Kevin into the service porch.

"What happened?" she asked.

"It's nothing," Dan said. "Just a little tumble off the fence. But he needs some TLC."

Once in the kitchen, the flavorful aroma of roast beef about knocked him to his knees. Dang, that woman could cook. If the meal tasted only half as good as it smelled, they were going to be in for a treat.

"Here," she said, "bring him over to the sink so I can clean him up and get a look at that chin."

Moments later, and after a whole lot of sweet talk and tenderness, the boy was nearly as good as new.

What would Dan have done without Eva here?

Sure, he would have managed. But he would have been uneasy—and awkward.

"Are you going to spend the night with us?" Kevin asked Eva. "I wish you would."

"I'm sorry, honey." She tossed away the damp paper towel she'd been using to clean his face. "I didn't bring any clothes or a toothbrush with me. So, after dinner, I'm going home."

"Then when are you coming back?" he prodded. "Will you be here tomorrow?"

"I have to work, but I can come again next weekend." She turned to Dan, and when she looked at him with those pretty brown eyes, he was toast.

And the old adage he'd been repeating to himself all afternoon? *Out of sight, out of mind?*

It faded in the wind.

Why couldn't he just tell Eva that it wasn't necessary for her to come out to the ranch anymore? Why didn't he say that he couldn't continue to take advantage of her good nature, that he would hire someone soon?

Before he could even venture a response, he got an elbow in the side and turned to see that Hank had somehow slipped beside him.

"Since Eva will be here to cook next weekend," the old man said, "I aim to take full advantage of that. What do you think about having a fish fry? You could take those kids down to the lake on Saturday and catch some catfish or maybe some bass."

Dan hadn't been fishing in ages; he hadn't had time. And as much as he'd like to find a couple hours out of his day, he couldn't take the kids.

Not without help.

"Maybe we ought to ask Eva what she thinks," Hank said, taking the option out of Dan's hand and handing it over to the woman who'd turned his world on end in a couple of days' time.

"About what?" Eva asked. "Fixing fish for dinner next Saturday?"

"Actually," Hank said, "Dan makes a great beer batter and can handle a flame and a skillet. So you'd only need to whip up the side dishes."

"I can certainly do that," Eva said.

Even if Dan felt comfortable being alone with the kids—and he *didn't*—he wasn't going to make plans that included Eva next weekend. Not when he was going to thank her for her services after dinner tonight and then send her on her way.

"I don't think it's a good idea," he finally said, hoping to come up with a good reason that didn't make him look like the bad guy.

"Why isn't it?" Hank asked.

Dan wasn't about to admit that he was afraid to take the kids on an outing like that. After all, what if one of them got hurt again—on his watch?

"I don't think the fish have been biting this summer," he said. Then, for good measure, he added, "And I'd really hate to disappoint the kids."

"Don't worry about Kevin and Kaylee," Eva said. "Something tells me they're going to love going to the lake with you, even if you don't catch a thing."

Now what? Dan wondered.

"I don't see a problem, either." Hank leaned against the kitchen counter, crossed his arms and smirked as though he had the entire day mapped out already. "If you come up empty handed, you can always stop at Miller's Market on the way home and buy some filets."

Apparently, Hank had his mind set on the fishing trip and wasn't going to let it drop.

"Okay," Dan told his uncle, agreeing against his better judgment. "But you're going with me and the kids to the lake. Someone has to teach them how to bait a hook and cast a line. And I'm not going to do it alone."

"Don't look at me," Hank said. "I can hardly even walk on flat terrain these days. I'd probably fall and break a hip down at the lake. So Eva's going to have to go with you."

The suggestion knocked Dan for a loop. Having dinner with her again was one thing. But spending the day down at the lake, too?

No, it wasn't a good idea—no matter how much he liked to fish. No matter how much he liked looking at her and hearing her voice.

"Sure," she said. "I'll give you some help with the kids. But I'm afraid you'll have three students. I've never fished before."

"Then maybe we ought to plan it for another day." Dan tossed her a smile.

"That's not necessary," she said. "I'm game if you are."

That wasn't what he meant—or what he'd expected.

A silly ain't-I-clever grin on Hank's face suggested the old man had orchestrated the whole damn thing.

And Dan wasn't sure how to backpedal or get out of it now.

Dinner, as anyone might have guessed from the aroma that had filled the house, was great. And Hank had raved about it, even after a second helping of dessert, lemon meringue pie that practically melted in the mouth.

Who would have guessed that a laboratory scientist could whip up such tasty dishes in the kitchen?

Now, as Dan helped Eva clear the table, she said, "It'll be bedtime soon. Do you want to oversee the kids' baths while I do the dishes?"

He would have tried to rush her out of the house, but what was the use? She'd be back next weekend, so he'd better get used to having her around, to studying her from a distance, to having her image slip into his mind when she was nowhere in sight.

"I'll do the dishes," he said. "You take the tub duties."

Eva smiled. "You've got a deal." Then she walked out of the kitchen, leaving him to his work.

A couple of minutes later, the phone rang. Dan wiped his hands, then answered, surprised to hear the voice of Jimmy Rawlings, an old buddy.

They chatted for a while, catching up on each other's lives, and by the time he'd wiped down the countertops and put the last dish away, Eva returned.

"That was easy," she said, looking a bit relieved.

"What was?"

"Tucking them in. They were exhausted. In fact, I tried to tell them a bedtime story, but they dozed off before I finished."

"Did they nap today?" he asked.

Her eyes widened, and her lips parted. "I didn't realize that they needed one."

"I only knew about their sleeping habits because their mother's roommate made a list for me before I left New York."

He'd expected her to smile, but something seemed

to be bothering her. "I'm sorry. I should have realized that, at their age, they needed to rest."

"Don't worry," he said, shaking it off. "For what it's worth, 'tucking them in at night' wasn't on the list. And maybe it should have been. But apparently, you had that one nailed."

"Maybe." She shrugged. "Whenever I stayed with my grandmother, she'd come in and sit on the bed for a while, and I liked it. So I figured Kaylee and Kevin would appreciate it, too."

"Did your mom tuck you in at night?"

"No. I really don't remember her."

Dan didn't remember his mother, either. Just a fleeting image here and there, none of which he could wrap his heart around. And the fact that he'd never known her had left a gap of some kind in his life that he'd never been able to close.

"Well," Eva said, as she scanned the kitchen, "I'd better head home. It's getting late." When she spotted her purse hanging on the back of a chair, she reached for it. "And to be honest, the kids aren't the only ones who had a big day."

"Thanks for helping out," he said, thinking he ought to be glad she was going and wondering why he wasn't.

"You're welcome." She fingered the shoulder strap of her purse, which tugged on her blouse, revealing more of her neck and the scar she tried to hide. "I really enjoyed it. The kids are great."

He tore his gaze from the damaged skin she tried to hide. While he wondered how it had happened, he would never ask.

As she made her way to the back door, he said, "I'll walk you out."

Her steps slowed to a stop, and she turned to face him. "You don't have to do that."

Sure he did. All he needed was for her to take a stumble in the dark again, which was the excuse he gave himself as he followed her out of the house into the yard and to her car.

Yet she didn't make any move toward opening the door. Instead, she leaned against it. "Thank you for letting me come out here and spend time with the kids. It's been good practice for me."

"Then it's a win-win for both of us. For the most part, I'm lost when it comes to dealing with them."

"Why do you say that?"

He shrugged. "I never really had a family."

"You had a sister."

"Yeah, but we were pretty much on our own as kids."

She stiffened, and her brow furrowed. "I'm sorry to hear that."

"Yeah, well, we dealt with it." But it hadn't been easy.

Eva didn't ask any more questions, which he appreciated. Some scars weren't the physical kind. Yet for some crazy reason, he found himself explaining anyway. "Our mother ran off—or so we were told—and our father had a serious gambling problem that kept us moving from place to place. So we had to fend for ourselves a lot of the time."

"How old were you?"

"Seven or eight, I guess. Then, one day, our old man drove us out here and left us with Hank." He paused as his mind rolled back to the early days on the ranch. "As one day blurred into the next, it became apparent that we'd been abandoned. Hank could have turned us over to social workers, but instead he provided us with a place to live without complaint."

Well, not much of one. One night, Dan had overheard Hank and Manuel talking. Hank had been cussing a blue streak about something, and his old man's name had come up, too. But before Dan could have gleaned anything more than that, Manuel had silently nodded toward the doorway where Dan had been standing, and Hank had shut up.

"Was Hank good to you?"

"In his own way. But we weren't used to his gruffness. Or living with his rules."

"What kind of rules?"

"Having chores and responsibilities each day, being accountable for our actions."

"That sounds like it might have been good for you."

"It was. And it didn't take long to realize he meant well and that he was more bark than bite. Before long, Jenny and I realized we had a better home than the one we'd had before."

"Did he tell you that he loved you?" Her gaze locked on his as though the answer mattered, as though it had been important.

"Not in so many words. And we didn't receive much in the way of physical affection, but we—or at least I—knew that he cared about me."

"Your sister didn't?"

"She was a girl, and I think Hank had a harder time relating to her." It was, Dan realized, the same with him and Kaylee. He cared about his niece more than anyone might know. He wanted her safe and happy, but he didn't know how to treat her, how to offer the affection that Jenny had always craved but had never gotten.

"Did your sister have a difficult time relating to Hank?"

"Yes, in a way. She was always into more cultural things like music and dancing and art." In fact, she'd spent all of her free time in her room with the door closed, books spread across her bed and the radio set on a classical station. "So, as you can probably guess, she and Hank had very little in common."

"And you took right to ranching?"

"That pretty much sums it up. I was a natural on horseback and loved working cattle." In fact, it was those skills that had made it easy for Dan to step up to the plate and to take over running the ranch when Hank had a heart attack.

"How'd your sister fit in?"

"She never really did. She always wanted a different life for herself. So she saved her allowance, and the day she turned eighteen, she flew to New York with hopes of landing a career on Broadway."

"Did she find what she was looking for?"

"I don't think so. She had talent, but she never quite made it to the big time. Then she got pregnant with the twins."

At one time, Dan and Jenny had been so close they'd been inseparable, but they'd fallen out of step, out of touch. And now she was gone completely. The only thing left were her kids and an occasional glimpse of her in their eyes, in their smiles, in their mannerisms.

"Did you know Kaylee and Kevin's father?" Eva asked.

"Nope. We never met. And from what I've been told, he was never a significant part of her or the children's lives."

Dan didn't see any reason to admit that he'd resented Jenny for leaving Texas. That it would have been nice to have someone on the ranch with whom he could talk in the evenings, someone with whom he could confide. Someone who cared about his own hopes and dreams, not that they were ever as lofty as Jenny's.

He was also reluctant to tell Eva that he and his sister had become estranged over the years, that he was sorry that he'd let their rift—which seemed very minor now—go on way too long.

"How about you?" he asked. "Do you have any brothers or sisters?"

"No." She glanced down at her feet, then back to his eyes. "It's just me."

In the moonlight, he caught a glimpse of something in her gaze—wistfulness? Sadness?

It was hard to say, but it touched him. And it caught him off guard.

"I get the feeling your life wasn't all that happy, either," he said.

She shook her head. "No, I grew up in a dysfunctional home, too. My mom had a serious drug problem, and my stepfather... Well, let's just say he was a jerk."

"Did he hurt you?" Dan wasn't sure why he asked. Just curious, he supposed.

"Sometimes, especially when he drank, he'd say cruel things. He had a temper, too, and hit me once in a while. But I managed to get by. I know of kids who had it worse."

That didn't make Dan feel any better. It angered him to think of Eva at the hands of a brute, someone who would hurt her in any way.

"I guess we had something in common," he said.

"What's that?"

"Lousy childhoods."

She pushed away from the car, standing a little taller. "But just because someone had a sad and lonely past doesn't mean they can't provide their own kids with a better life than they had."

She had a point there, he supposed. But that didn't make him feel any better about his parenting skills—or the lack thereof. He feared that he wouldn't do right by his niece and nephew, that they'd run off someday, too.

He glanced at the corral, at the railing where Kevin had climbed earlier. The thought that the agile little boy might fall hadn't crossed Dan's mind, and he blamed himself for not seeing the accident coming.

Isn't that what he'd observed and overheard at the park that day he'd gone to the Parents of Multiples picnic?

Some of those parents seemed to have a sixth sense when it came to dealing with their kids. And that psychic ability or whatever it was that helped them to avoid the inevitable. Even now, he could hear some of their voices.

Get away from your brother while he's swinging, Jonathon.

Don't pester that older boy, Kara.

Wash your hands before you eat.

He shook off the voices that reminded him he didn't have the foresight needed—or anything else, for that matter.

"I'd like to be a good dad to the twins," he admitted, "even if I never had a decent role model or planned to be a father myself. But I'm so out of my element, especially with Kaylee, that I'm worried I'm going to screw up."

And for a man who'd never felt insecure in his life, that was a pretty big admission.

He glanced down at the scuffed toes of his boots. When he looked up and caught her eye, he found her gazing at him as though she'd found something to admire—some skill he might not have noticed.

"The kids adore you," she said.

Her words took him aback. "How do you know that?"

"Kevin really looks up to you. In fact, he talked about you all day long. And Kaylee said you were more handsome than Prince Charming."

There went all that make-believe stuff again. The fantasy that Eva created to help the medicine go down.

The fact that she'd tried to swing things his way was nice, but he knew the reality. His only parental role model had been Hank, and as decent as the old rancher had been in a lot of ways, he'd never quite connected with Jenny, never quite managed to make her consider the ranch her home.

"You know," Eva said, "I could come and help out for a little while. I've got some vacation time I really need to take."

"Don't you want to save it and use it when you have the babies?"

"I'd love to, but I've accrued so many hours that it's one of those use-it-or-lose-it deals. But don't worry. I'll still have plenty when the baby comes." The night breeze blew a loose strand of hair across her cheek, and she brushed it aside. "Why don't I see what I can do? If I can schedule the time, I could stay here for a week or so until you hire someone permanent."

She was offering to be a temporary nanny?

Dan liked the idea much more than he dared to admit, but he was afraid to jump on her suggestion for a very good reason—his growing attraction to her. His game plan had been to send her on her way before he started to like having her around too much. So a part of him wanted to tell her he'd be just fine on his own.

But he wasn't so sure about that. And right this minute, he wasn't in that big of a rush to chase her off. Not with her standing before him, her gaze setting him on edge, his pulse doing weird things as a result.

The breeze kicked up again, stirring more than the air around them, more than her floral scent.

And then it happened again, that soul-stirring urge to wrap his arms around her and kiss her senseless.

He'd fought it the first time, but he wasn't sure if he could do it again. Hell, he wasn't sure if he even wanted to try.

To make matters worse, she seemed to be caught up in the same invisible web that he was, one that was drawing them, pulling them, binding them....

She didn't say a word, didn't need to. Even in the moonlight he could see the writing on the wall.

She wanted a kiss as badly as he did.

Heaven help him when it was all over, but he couldn't resist any longer. Tossing aside any and all reservations, he cupped her jaw, his fingers grazing the damaged skin, and lowered his mouth to hers.

He'd meant it to be a simple kiss. But as her lips parted, as he stole a taste of her, the stars in the evening sky seemed to burst into fireworks.

His tongue sought hers, found it, and desire flared, tempting him, taunting him. He drew her tighter, kissed her deeper.

His hands slid along her back and hips, exploring every curve, every inch. He wasn't sure what was happening or what he'd do about it when it was all said and done, but for now, he claimed what seemed to be his.

As the kiss intensified, she whimpered and leaned into him, holding on as if she might collapse if she didn't. And for a moment, he wondered just how steady he'd be on his feet if either of them let go.

Damn. What in blazes was he thinking?

He slowly removed his mouth from hers, and as their ragged breaths mingled in the night air, he considered letting go and taking a step back.

Instead, he continued to hold her until he was sure she'd stay upright, until he was sure he'd be able to stand firm, too. When he felt her steady, he took a step back.

"I...uh..." He raked a hand through his hair. "I'm sorry about that. I don't know what got into me."

Her cheeks appeared flushed, or maybe that was just his imagination.

"I don't usually do things like that, either," she said.

Like what? Kiss men she hardly knew?

Heck, that might be true. She'd even gone the test-tube route when it came to conception. But he wasn't about to let the conversation go there.

"I won't let that happen again," he said.

"It's okay," she said, her voice soft, sultry, maybe even shy. "Don't give it another thought."

But it *wasn't* okay. Not if Dan was determined not to have a romantic relationship with the kids' babysitter. And while Eva might only be a temporary nanny, she was also pregnant—no need to forget that.

And as for not giving it another thought, it seemed to be front and center on his mind right now, and something told him the memory of that kiss was going to dog him for the rest of the week.

"I really ought to go," she said.

Clearly, that was their best option at this point.

He opened the car door for her and waited for her to slip behind the wheel.

"Drive careful," he said. "And thanks."

She tossed him a pretty smile, then turned on the ignition. After she locked herself safely inside, he stepped away from the vehicle and watched her drive away.

What was he going to do now? She'd be back on Saturday—with an overnight bag. He could, of course, call her during the week and tell her something had come up, that he wouldn't need her to stay with him after all.

But then he thought of the corral, of Kevin's fall earlier today. The boy hadn't been hurt seriously, but something like that was bound to happen again. Kevin was active. And curious.

And Dan was *so* inexperienced.

Kaylee's stitches…

Kevin's scraped chin, the split lip...

What would happen next?

Dan feared the questions would continue to play over and over in his head for the next five days. And if he didn't find a permanent nanny quick, he'd have to take what Eva was offering.

He just hoped to hell that he wasn't tempted to take more than that.

Chapter Six

Dan couldn't believe that he'd agreed to let Eva come and stay at the ranch for two whole weeks.

He probably should have called and told her not to come, that he'd already put an ad in the local newspaper, seeking a housekeeper/sitter. That it was just a matter of time before he found the perfect person. But in truth, his advertisement came out on Tuesday, and he still hadn't gotten a single response.

What was with that? Weren't there any potential babysitters in town? Were they all happily employed by other families?

Dan had asked Hank what he thought about the lack of response, and the old man had merely smirked. "Guess it just ain't meant to be."

"What isn't?"

"Finding someone else to cook and clean for us."

"The cooking is secondary," Dan had said. "The

woman I hire will be taking care of the kids, not you and me."

His uncle had merely picked up a *Today's Cattleman* magazine from the coffee table and thumbed through it.

Apparently, he just didn't get it.

Dan glanced at the clock on the mantel. Eva would be here soon, so he might as well go out to the barn and get the fishing gear for a trip that had him feeling awkward and uneasy before they'd even climbed into the truck.

Jack, the cattle dog, met him in the yard, tail swishing, then followed him into the barn. The dog seemed oblivious to the puppies that nested in the straw with their mother.

There were some things that were better left to the females of the species, Dan thought. And even a dog knew that.

As he gathered four poles together, as well as a tackle box, he cursed under his breath.

What would Eva be expecting from him after that kiss they'd shared on Sunday night?

She'd told him to forget about it, of course. And they'd gone five days without talking at all. So maybe she hadn't thought anything of it and had disregarded the whole thing.

He sure hoped so because he wasn't up for any of those "Now what?" and "Where do we go from here?" discussions.

As he carried the fishing gear out of the barn, he ran into Manuel, who'd just climbed out of his Ford pickup.

"What are you doing?" the old cowboy asked as he glanced at the gear Dan held.

"Just getting the fishing poles."

Manuel furrowed his brow. "You taking the day off?"

Dan's movements froze. "Is there anything wrong with that?"

"No, not at all. It just surprised me, that's all."

"Well, for what it's worth, it's more like work than pleasure. I'm taking Eva and the kids to the lake."

"Oh," Manuel said, nodding as though it now made perfect sense. "Hank said she was going to stay here for a couple of weeks."

Dan gave a little shrug. "We can't expect her to make the drive back and forth each day."

The grin Manuel had been wearing stretched into a playful smirk. "So she'll be staying with you in the house? *Overnight?*"

"What's wrong with that?"

"Nothing. She seems like a mighty fine houseguest to me."

Dan scoffed. Manuel had been married twice. His first wife had died, but he hadn't stayed single very long. About six months later, he had tied the knot again. And for some reason, he seemed to think everyone ought to be hitched.

"Don't worry about me," Dan said. "I'm not like you, *compadre*."

"Oh, no?"

Dan clucked his tongue and made his way to the porch, where he planned to check the tackle box and see what he'd need to pick up at the bait shop. He hadn't fished in ages. Under normal circumstances, he'd be looking forward to a leisurely day at the lake, but he expected that taking the kids and Eva would be a real chore.

There'd been a part of him that had wished Eva would forget more than just the kiss they'd had. He actually hoped that she would forget to show up at all.

But when he heard a vehicle approach and spotted Eva's car kicking up dust along the drive, he knew that wasn't going to happen.

It had taken Eva a couple of days to square away her schedule at work so that she'd be able to take time off, but it had finally come together. She'd hoped to start her vacation by Wednesday or Thursday, but that would have left the lab shorthanded. As a result, she'd had to finish out the week.

On Friday night, she'd done a little Internet research and learned that many fishermen liked to start out early in the day, so she'd set her alarm for dawn. She'd also packed her bags, although finding clothing to take with her hadn't been an easy job. Her waistline was filling out by leaps and bounds, and a lot of her pants didn't fit anymore. At the rate she was going, she'd have to plan a shopping trip for herself between now and the time she left the ranch.

But she was looking forward to moving in with the kids more than she could have imagined.

Okay, so part of her excitement had to do with seeing Dan again. The memory of his kiss was still buzzing in her mind.

She'd been kissed before, but never like that. It had

nearly lifted her right out of her shoes. And the closer she got to the ranch, the more she thought about it.

As she drove near the barn, she spotted Manuel in the yard and Dan on the porch. Both men stopped to watch her park, but it was Dan's attention she sought.

She'd no more than opened the car door when the kids dashed outside to greet her, forcing her to focus on them instead. But wasn't that how it should be?

"We fixed up a room for you to stay in," Kaylee said. "I told Uncle Dan you could be in my room with me, but he said you want to have your own bedroom."

Eva hadn't given the sleeping arrangements much thought until that very moment. And when the porch flooring creaked, and she spotted Dan stepping down into the yard and heading her way, her bedtime visions took an unexpected turn toward satin sheets, soft music and moonlight wafting through gossamer curtains.

"Do you need any help?" he asked.

"If you don't mind. Thanks. My bag's in the back-seat. I also packed a lunch for us to take the lake. It's in the cooler, which is right next to an old quilt we can use to sit on while we eat."

Dan managed to grab all three of the items before she could tell him she'd carry one of them.

"Why don't I show you your room?" he said.

"All right."

He left the cooler and the quilt on the porch next to the fishing gear, then led her into the house.

There they went again, thoughts of bedtime, of removing clothes and turning off lights.

As she followed Dan down the hall, she shook off the inappropriate musing and scolded herself for letting her mind wander.

This was *so* not about her. And it wasn't about him, either. She was here for the twins—his, as well as hers.

"I'm afraid all the upstairs bedrooms are taken," he said. "And I apologize for this one being so small."

"That's okay. I wouldn't have minded sleeping on the sofa."

He paused halfway down the hall, his gaze snagging hers. The intensity, the sincerity in his gaze caused her heart to flip-flop as he said, "I'd give up my own bed before I'd do that to you."

"I wouldn't take yours."

His expression seemed to ask, "Why not?" But she wouldn't allow the conversation to drift in that direction, not when her thoughts kept straying as it was.

For the first time since she'd offered to stay with Dan and the kids and help him out, she began to question the wisdom of doing so.

He took a couple more steps, then stopped beside a doorway and made an after-you motion with his hand. "Here it is."

She passed through the threshold and into a room that was so small it could barely contain a double bed and a nightstand. But someone had placed a bud vase holding a pink geranium on the nightstand.

The welcoming gesture was heartwarming. She turned to say so just as Dan stepped through the doorway with her bag.

They stood face-to-face with very little distance between them. She should have felt uneasy, boxed in by a man so large—and she did, somewhat. But her overall uneasiness didn't seem to come from fear.

"I really feel badly about this room," he said.

"Why?"

"It isn't much bigger than a broom closet." He tossed her a boyish grin that turned her heart on end. "But at least you'll have some privacy. And, hopefully, some peace and quiet when you need it."

There was that upside, she supposed—if she closed the door. But the room didn't feel the least bit private or quiet right now.

Could he hear her heart pounding?

"This is perfect," she said, shaking it all off—the size of the room, the woodsy scent of his cologne that bore a hint of leather and musk, the female hormones that seemed to be running amok. She offered up a smile. "Really."

They stood like that for a beat, not moving one way or the other, not speaking.

Something warm and vital buzzed around her, although she'd be darned if she knew what it was. She tried to come up with a clever comment or a humorous quip of some kind, but she'd never been very good at chitchat, so she found herself stumped.

Fortunately, the kids came to the doorway, taking the heat off Eva and setting things back to rights.

As Kevin and Kaylee chattered among themselves about fishing trips, first grade and the big playground at the school they would attend in September. Dan wondered if Eva was as thankful for the interruption as he was. For a moment, he'd gotten caught up in thoughts that had nothing to do with kids or nannies and everything to do with men and women.

"Uncle Dan, can we take Eva outside and show her the puppies?" Kevin asked.

"Sure—if she wants to see them."

"Jill's babies are getting big," Kaylee explained. "You should see them now. They're really cute."

Eva set her purse on the bed. "I'd love to see them."

"Then come on." Kaylee reached out her hand.

Dan pressed his back against the wall, letting Eva pass by him and watching the twins take the attractive brunette away.

He couldn't help but blow out a sigh of relief. Eva had stirred up something inside of him just moments ago, leaving him uneasy with her presence. And instead of being relieved to have her help, as he'd hoped he would be, he was now perplexed by it.

Over the years, the ranch had always been his refuge, the place he went to find balance and peace, where he could always be himself. And now all of that was about to change.

He tried to remind himself that Eva being here was a good thing, that the positive repercussions of their temporary situation outweighed the bad. After all, she was better equipped to deal with the kids than he was.

On top of that, she'd lifted Kaylee's spirits, freeing the poor little girl from the depression that had dogged her since moving to Texas. He had a feeling that Kaylee had recognized something in Eva that had reminded her of her mom, and the two seemed to have forged an almost instant bond. So that was worth any awkwardness Dan might feel.

Hey, he reminded himself. *Two weeks really isn't very long.* And with Eva taking care of the kids' day-to-day needs, Dan was free to focus on running the ranch and all that entailed. Besides, by the time her vacation time was over, he hoped to have found someone permanent to help with childcare, someone who could provide the kids with all their emotional needs.

So as the twins took Eva outside to check on the litter of pups in the barn, Dan placed her bag at the foot of the bed. He wasn't used to having a woman live in such close proximity. His dates and relationships, for obvious reasons, had all been off the ranch. But he'd make the best of it.

Not that this thing with Eva could be construed as a relationship or that she could be considered a potential date.

Okay, so someone had to convince his hormones of that. Eva was clearly off-limits, even though her presence was having an arousing effect on him and sent his blood pumping in all the right places.

Having her around was certainly going to complicate his life over the next two weeks, but he could handle it.

What other choice did he have? But he'd be damned if he'd risk getting romantically involved with her.

On his way through the living room and out of the house, he spotted a colorful Lego structure Kevin had been building earlier, a mess by the hearth he'd apparently forgotten about. Dan would ask him to clean it up before they left for the lake.

He headed outside and gathered up the fishing gear, which he'd left on the porch. After packing it in the back of the truck, he returned for the quilt and the cooler. But on his way back to the pickup, curiosity soon overtook him, and he decided to take a peek at the lunch Eva had made for them.

So, after placing the insulated container in the

bed of the truck, he lifted the lid and spotted home-made oatmeal cookies, pretzels, sliced oranges and sandwiches.

God, he hoped they weren't bologna.

He picked up one of the plastic-wrap baggies and noted that at least one of them was peanut butter and jelly. Dang, he might have to fight one of the kids for that. He liked bologna as much as the next guy, but since Hank considered that particular lunchmeat part of the basic food groups, Dan had tolerated more than his share of it over the years.

"I packed ham and cheese for us," Eva said, drawing his attention as she and the kids walked out of the barn.

Feeling a little too much like a kid who was caught reaching into a cookie jar, Dan closed up the cooler and stepped away from the truck.

"I hope that's okay with you," Eva said. "I could go into the house and look for some—"

"No, don't do that. Ham and cheese sounds great."

The screen door squeaked open, and as Hank stepped out onto the porch, he hollered, "Where's my cane? Did one of you little hooligans take it again? How many times do I have to tell you? That's not a toy!"

"Oops," Kevin said, as he trotted toward the house. "I'll get it for you. I had to borrow it to get something out from under the bed. And the hook on the end is a good catcher."

"Well, you should have asked me, boy."

"You were sleeping, Uncle Hank. And I didn't want to wake you up."

As the boy ran into the house, Hank snorted. "That kid is going to be the death of me."

"I'm sorry he borrowed your cane without asking," Dan said. "I'll talk to him about it while we're gone and make sure he doesn't borrow your things without permission again."

The old man merely grumbled.

Moments later, Kevin returned with the cane and handed it to the old cowboy, who took it and put it to good use.

"The bass won't be biting much longer," Hank said. "And I got my heart set on a fish fry tonight. When are you leaving?"

"As soon as Kevin cleans up his mess in the living room," Dan said.

"I'll do it right now," the boy said, as he dashed back into the house.

His sister tagged after him, apparently planning to help.

"Are you sure you don't want to go with us?" Eva asked Hank. "We can take a chair so you can sit in the shade."

"Not today. I'd better stick close to the house."

"Why?" Dan asked. "Are you feeling okay?"

The old man covered his mouth, then hacked and coughed. "That...blasted...en-suh-feemia is acting up."

"The doctor gave you that oxygen for a reason. I hope that means you plan to use it today."

Hank snorted, then turned and headed back to the house, his cane providing him support. As he stepped onto the porch, a coughing spasm overtook him.

Eva lowered her voice and spoke to Dan. "Did he mean emphysema?"

"Yeah. I'm afraid that years of smoking have taken

a real toll on him. But don't bother correcting his pronunciation. He's been told a hundred times, and I think he gets it wrong on purpose. It seems to be his way of rebelling against the diagnosis."

"Is he that stubborn?"

"He's the worst when he decides to dig in his heels about something." Dan leaned his hip against the side of the truck and studied Eva.

She was wearing jeans today, with a pink blouse that wasn't tucked in. Her dark hair was woven in a fancy braid that hung down her back, which was probably a good style for hiking along the lake, but he wished she'd worn it loose. He'd always been partial to women with long, silky tresses, and Eva in particular, it seemed.

"I feel sorry for Hank," she said.

So did Dan, but that was because, in his prime, he'd once been a tough-as-rawhide cowboy. Seeing his uncle stooped, aged and frail was tough. But he was curious about Eva's reasons for sympathy. "Why do you say that?"

"I suppose it's because I have a soft spot for the elderly."

That still surprised him, although he didn't know why it would. She was good with kids, so it made sense.

"Do you think he'll be okay while we're gone?" she asked.

"Probably, but I'll have Manuel check on him." Dan scanned the yard, eager to get on the road. "I wonder what's keeping the kids. It shouldn't take them very long to pick up those Legos and put them away."

"They're probably looking for their swimsuits, although I told them they'd have to talk to you about that. Is it okay? Is the lake safe for swimming?"

He forgot that she was a lab technologist and that she might be worried about bacteria and germs, but he didn't want to raise the kids in a bubble. "It'll be okay. I'm of the mind that a little dirt on the hands and mud between the toes is good for kids."

Minutes later, the kids ran out the backdoor, where Jack met them, tail wagging as if he knew they were headed for an adventure and he wanted to be included.

"We're ready to go," Kevin said, pausing to pet the dog and give his ears a little rub. "Can Jack and Jill go with us?"

"Not Jill," Kaylee corrected. "She has to stay with her babies, remember?"

"Oh, yeah."

Dan tousled the boy's hair. "Sure, why not. We'd probably have to tie him up to keep him from following us."

As the kids and Eva climbed into the pickup, Dan lowered the tailgate and let the dog jump in back. Then he climbed behind the wheel and started up the engine, as the pickup roared to life.

In the back, Jack let out a happy bark.

"It's fun having a real family again," Kevin said.

Dan wasn't sure what the boy meant by "again." As far as he knew, his sister's kids had never lived in a two-parent home, which was what Dan would consider a "real" family.

And a trip to the lake with his uncle and a temporary nanny didn't even come close to the real deal, even if they all looked the part—down to the dog in the back of the truck.

He shot a glance across the seat at Eva, saw what appeared to be a wistful smile on her face and suspected she'd gotten a kick out of the kid's comment.

Hopefully, no one really expected them to have a typical Norman Rockwell outing today. He'd give a day at the lake his best shot, though.

He just hoped no one was disappointed in the process.

Chapter Seven

Cottonwood Lake was located on a grassy, parklike stretch of land not far from the ranch. And while there were a couple of men fishing on the other side, Eva, Dan and the kids pretty much had the place to themselves.

From what Dan had mentioned during lunch, Hank had owned the property originally. About twenty years ago, he'd dammed the creek that fed into it, increasing the size. Then he'd stocked it with bass. But when his wife, Millie, had gotten ill, he'd had to sell the property to pay her extensive medical bills. The county park and recreation department purchased it from him and made it into a community park.

Both Hank and Dan loved to fish and came out here whenever they could get away. But Dan hadn't been having much luck today.

Eva had given fishing a try earlier this morning, but like the kids, she'd gotten bored after a while and had called it a day. Now she sat on the old quilt and relished the sounds of nature and happy children at play.

"It's pretty out here," she said, noting the nearby cottonwoods, hearing the sounds of a blue jay calling to its mate, feeling the warmth of the sun upon her face.

"I think so, too." Dan cast his line again. "It's a nice place to slip away and think."

She watched the handsome cowboy, who'd shed his hat and boots and looked more like an outdoorsman right now than a rancher. His smile, which he'd tossed her way several times today, was more carefree than she'd ever seen before.

Fishing, she decided, was good for him.

And watching him seemed to be good for her, too.

Every now and then, Dan would glance over his shoulder at her, as though making sure she was still there. A couple of times, she'd noticed something else in his expression, a spark of some kind, an intensity that nearly turned her heart on end.

She wondered if he was thinking about the kiss they'd shared, even if neither of them had ever mentioned it again. Even if it seemed as though it had never really happened.

But she knew better. It hadn't been a dream. No way could she have imagined something so heart-stirring that it had promised to change her entire outlook on life.

Okay, so she wasn't exactly sure what had happened inside of her that night, but something had—so much so that she'd been afraid to mention it again.

But why was Dan pretending that he'd never wrapped his arms around her, drawn her close and kissed her senseless?

There was only one conclusion she could come to. Her pregnancy must have doused whatever heat that had surged through them, at least as far as Dan was concerned.

He hadn't made any secret of the fact that he had his hands full with his sister's twins. Two more would probably throw his life into turmoil. So why in the world would a man who'd never been married want to take on more children than he could handle?

Not that she was making the jump from a kiss to a relationship. But isn't that what sometimes happened?

Still, as the kids frolicked on the shoreline, their skin glistening with the sunblock she'd applied earlier, her attention was drawn to them and the dog.

Kevin laughed and threw a stick for Jack to chase, and Kaylee clapped her hands as the dog took off.

It was hard not to see them as a blessing, as a wonderful addition to their uncle's life.

And they would be to *anyone's* life, she realized. They'd certainly been a blessing to her in the short time she'd known them.

Earlier, Kevin had said it was nice being a family again. Eva had bitten her tongue when he'd made the comment, but she'd wanted to agree. She might not have had the same loving family experience that the kids had obviously had, but she was able to catch a glimpse of "normal" just by being here with them today.

Other than the short time she'd spent with her *abuelita,* who'd been the kind of woman Eva planned to emulate, her own childhood and life experience had been sorely lacking. So just being with Dan and the kids had given her a glimpse of the home and family she'd always dreamed of having.

But as she'd learned in the past, nothing lasted forever.

"Well," Dan said, as he reeled in his line. "Looks like we'll need to go to the market and purchase some fillets after all. Unless you want me to pick up some take-out from Honey's Café. She has a nice fish-and-chips plate."

"I don't want to disappoint Hank," Eva said, "so I vote for the fillets. That is, if you don't mind fixing them. I've got recipes for some side dishes I'd like to make."

"Then that's what we'll do. You haven't tasted anything like my beer-battered fish."

He made it sound like a piece of cake, but she suspected that moving about the kitchen and working in such close proximity with him might not be that easy. But she let the subject drop, even if her thoughts remained on this evening's dinner prep.

And bumping elbows—or whatever—in the kitchen.

That evening, while Kaylee and Kevin watched television, Dan and Eva worked together fixing dinner. The kids had played their hearts out at the lake, and even Jack had been too pooped to wag his tail when they got home.

As Dan moved through the kitchen, whipping up his special beer batter and heating up the cast-iron skillet, he had a hard time keeping his eyes off the pretty brunette, who was chopping cucumbers for a salad.

She looked a little tired, and her cheeks were a bit flushed. He wished he hadn't taken her up on her suggestion that she make the side dishes.

"Are you sure you don't want to take some time to put your feet up?" he asked.

"I'm fine. I didn't do much today." She offered him a smile that reached deep inside of him, catching him off guard and leaving him at a loss.

Why did he have the need to watch her, to protect her?

Fortunately, Hank joined them in the kitchen, giving Dan something else to think about.

"So what kind of fillets did you pick up?" the old cowboy asked as he neared the stove.

"Halibut." Dan lit the flame under the skillet and poured in some oil. "Are you okay with that?"

"I had my heart set on bass, but I'll live."

Hank, who'd become even more crotchety after his stroke, sidled up to Eva. "What have you got there?"

"A garden salad. But in a moment, I'm going to start making rice pilaf. It's a recipe I got from my friend, Clara Morrison. And she said it's really tasty."

Hank perked up. "I know a woman by that name, but she's probably too old to be a friend of yours."

"It's probably the same woman," Eva said. "Clara is in her seventies and has lived near Brighton Valley her entire life."

"No kidding?" The old man stroked his bristled chin. "Where'd you meet her?"

"At the senior center. I volunteer there."

"You don't say. How's she doing? I haven't seen her in close to twenty years."

"She's doing great, as far as her health goes. But her husband died last year, so she's been a little lonely. She's doing better, though. She's getting used to being a widow. Playing cards at the center has helped her get out more and make new friends."

"That's too bad about her husband," Dan said to Eva before turning his attention to Hank. "Wasn't he a history teacher at the high school?"

Hank grimaced.

"I think he was," Eva said. "Clara made some comment about him being a history nut."

Hank humphed. "He was a *nut,* all right."

"What's that supposed to mean?" Dan asked, not that it mattered. But it was obvious his uncle wasn't keen on Mr. Morrison, who'd been one of Jenny's teachers, but not one of his.

Hank crossed his arms and frowned. "I never had much use for the guy."

Dan glanced at Eva, realizing he wasn't the only one who'd sensed something surly in Hank's tone, in his attitude. And now his curiosity was piqued. "Why's that?"

"It doesn't matter. I just didn't like him, that's all. But when he gave your sister a D on that big project she did when she was a senior, I went down to the school and complained."

Dan hadn't been aware of that, although he remembered his sister crying over her grade on a history project. She'd been hoping for an A in the class and seemed to think a scholarship hung in the balance.

"Who'd you complain to?" he asked his uncle.

"The principal, Ralph Hidalgo. I told him that Morrison had a thing against me and was taking it out on my niece, trying to punish her. Things got a little heated, and Hidalgo threatened to call the police if I came down to the school kicking up a fuss again."

Hank definitely could get out of sorts when he felt wronged, but he wouldn't hurt anyone.

"What did Mr. Morrison have against you?" Dan asked, realizing his uncle had managed to stir up trouble without him knowing anything about it.

"It was after I'd come home from Korea and he was just a mama's boy who was living at home and majoring in history in college. I told him I was going to kick his ass all the way back to prehistoric times if he didn't stay away from Clara." A silly grin stole across Hank's face, and he winked, his eyes twinkling. "And I would have done it, too. If Clara hadn't asked me to back off."

"So you two had a crush on the same girl," Dan said.

"Don't get me wrong," Hank said, more to Eva than to Dan. "I'm glad that things worked out the way they did. I loved Millie. But Clara and I dated before I went in the Army, and she dumped me for George Morrison while I was in Korea."

Eva placed a hand on Hank's shoulder. "I suppose that was her loss, wasn't it?"

He humphed again. "Clara thought I was a hellion and would never settle down, but she was wrong. A man can make all kinds of changes when he has the love and support of a good woman."

"So you each married other people," Eva said, voicing the obvious.

Hank nodded slowly, brow furrowed, his eyes averted. "And it all turned out for the best. Millie was a real sweetheart. And I doubt Clara would have put up with much of my nonsense."

The old man continued to stand there, his head lowered as though deep in thought. Then he turned and walked away.

When Hank was gone and out of earshot, Eva lowered her voice and said, "That's amazing. And kind of sad."

Dan had been a little blown away by it, too. He'd lived with Hank for more than twenty-five years, and he'd never known any of this. "My aunt died before Jenny and I came to live here, so I never really knew her. But Hank used to talk about her all the time, so I know he really cared about her."

"I'm sure he did."

Dan glanced at Eva, saw her gentle, knowing smile. But he could also see the cogs turning, the ones that put a glimmer in a woman's eye.

"Don't get carried away," he said. "I have a feeling that the only thing that's been simmering over the past sixty years was the grudge Hank held against Mr. Morrison, not the torch he carried for his wife."

"You're probably right." Eva leaned against the kitchen counter and crossed her arms, yet he suspected the cogs continued to move. "But did you see how introspective he got when Clara's name came up? I'll bet he still thinks about her every now and then."

"You're not getting any ideas, are you?"

Eva laughed, the lilt of her voice skimming along Dan's chest like a lover's fingers. Taunting, tempting.

"I'll bet seeing Clara again would improve his mood," Eva said.

"I doubt it." Then, half joking, half not, Dan added, "Hank can be a real bear sometimes."

"I know," Eva said, "but he's a likable bear."

That he was, and it surprised him that Eva had seen through the old man so quickly.

As Dan studied the compassion in her pretty brown eyes, he realized that she was just the kind of woman Hank had been talking about, the kind whose love and support could change a man.

It made Dan wonder, just for a moment, what kind of transformation Eva might make in him.

Of course, that was beside the point. He might have been forced to make a few changes in his life because of the kids, but at thirty-eight years old, he was too happy—and too damn set in his ways—to let a woman work on him.

No matter how pretty she was.

Eva had never taken part in a fish fry before, but she could certainly see why Hank would suggest they have one tonight. Dan's beer batter was to die for, and the halibut was especially light and tasty.

As she began to clear the table, Kevin asked, "Hey, when is Halloween?"

Where had that question come from? she wondered. But before she could answer him, his uncle did.

"It's in October, which is still a couple of months away." Dan looked at Eva and winked, then turned back to Kevin. "Are you planning your costume already?"

"No. It's just because me and Kaylee get to have a birthday when it's Halloween time, so I wanted to know how long we have to wait to be six."

"I remember when I used to look forward to birthdays." Hank chuckled. "Now I just try to forget them."

Kaylee placed her napkin on her plate. "How old are you, Uncle Hank? Are you a hundred?"

The elderly man cracked a smile. "Just about, missy. And some days I feel older than that."

Eva hadn't volunteered at the center long before she realized that many seniors dealt with more than their fair share of aches and pains.

"Cool," Kevin said. "You need a really big cake to hold all those candles."

"That's right." Hank stood and pushed his chair away from the table. "Lucky for me, I quit counting a long time ago."

"That's okay," Dan said, a glimmer in his eye. "I've been keeping track for you. On September tenth, you'll be seventy-eight."

Hank chuffed. "Thanks, kid. You're a real peach."

"When is that?" Kevin asked. "Is September tenth a long time from now?"

"Actually," Eva said, realizing they'd have to do something to celebrate, "his birthday is only about two weeks away."

"Hey!" Kevin brightened. "We can have a party for you!"

"Oh, no, you don't," Hank barked. "I don't want a party."

"Not even cake and ice cream?" Kaylee asked, her eyes big and hopeful.

As the old man looked at the sweet child, Eva watched his gruff exterior crack and soften.

"Well," he said, "I'd never turn down dessert, especially if it's something chocolate. But *no* candles! Otherwise, we'd have to call in the fire department to make sure we didn't burn down the house."

"Don't worry about a thing," Eva said, realizing she'd still be at the ranch when the big day came. "We'll just have chocolate cake for dessert on the tenth of September, and I'll make a fudge frosting. How about that?"

"I won't fight you on that." Hank pushed his chair back in place and stepped away from the table. "But no party. Got it?"

Eva tossed him an acquiescent smile, but her mind swirled with other ways they could celebrate.

"All right then." Hank turned to Kevin and Kaylee. "Why don't you two come along with me? We've got a movie set on Pause, and I want to see how it's going to end."

When the kids left with Hank, Dan and Eva made quick work of the cleanup. But all the while, her imagination took flight, and by the time she'd drained the sink and wrung out the dishcloth, her plan had come together.

"I'd like to have a little party for Hank on the tenth," she said.

"Are you kidding? You heard what he said."

"Yes, but he didn't mean it. I'm sure of it. Besides, we'll keep it small—and a surprise." There were a lot of little things she could do to make the evening special without going overboard.

Dan seemed to ponder her suggestion for a moment, then asked, "Who are you planning to invite?"

"Just Manuel and his wife. That's about it. Nothing too big or fancy."

Dan shrugged. "Sure, why not?"

With him on her side, the wheels really began to turn. "What would he like for dinner? What's his favorite meal?"

"Well, besides pot roast, he's big on turkey and all the fixings. He makes a point of going to Honey's Café on Thanksgiving and raves about it for months afterward."

Eva could get some pointers from Betsy. Or maybe even from Clara. "That sounds perfect. I'll whip up some stuffing, too, and mashed potatoes and gravy. What do you think about green beans and slivered almonds?"

"Sounds good to me." Dan flashed her a smile that turned her heart inside out.

"I'm going to make a chocolate cake," she said. "But in spite of his no-candle rule, I think we should have some anyway."

Dan, who'd folded the dishtowel and was setting it aside, paused. "You're planning to use seventy-eight candles?"

"No, we don't have to do that. Maybe just a few. Or I can pick up some of the ones that are shaped like numbers and use a seven and an eight."

"That would work without us having to invite the fire department." Dan grinned as he placed the towel on the counter, making Eva feel as though they'd become a team.

"Would you like a cup of coffee?" she asked, wanting the sense of unity to last.

"No, thanks. I think I'll turn in early. But first I need to head outside and make sure the barn is locked down for the night."

"I'll oversee the kids' baths. Then I'll take a shower and do some reading before bed."

"I'd like an early night, too."

Their gazes locked for a beat, as though neither was ready to go their separate ways.

Or was that only her imagination?

Why did she find herself reading into every word he said, into every glance he sent her way?

Finally, he said, "Sleep tight."

She nodded, then headed for the door into the living room, wishing there were still dishes to wash, dry and put away.

Behind her, Dan's boot steps sounded on the service porch flooring, then the backdoor opened to the yard.

"Oh, wow," he said. "Would you look at that?"

Curious—and glad to have an excuse to hang out with him for a little bit longer—Eva turned back and joined him at the railing on the porch.

He lifted his arm, and her gaze followed his pointed finger to the new moon, a huge white orb that nearly took her breath away.

She didn't think she'd ever seen one quite so large, so bright. It was almost mystical.

"It's beautiful," she said.

The night was still and quiet, even for a ranch. As they continued to stand there, caught up in the enchantment of a full moon, the whisper of Dan's scent—something musky and masculine—taunted her, making the moon and stars even more of a treat.

"You know," she said, "If I didn't have to supervise bath time, I'd sit out here for a few minutes and enjoy the view."

"The kids are okay for a while. What's the rush?"

"I guess there isn't one."

"Once I check out the barn, I'll join you—unless you'd rather be alone."

She'd spent way too much time by herself in the past to suit even the most hardened loner. "No, having company would be nice."

Minutes later, they were both seated on the porch steps, listening to a cricket chirp and a horse whinny in the field. Eva couldn't help thinking that this was one of the prettiest moons she could ever recall seeing.

But it was more than that making the night special. It was the man seated beside her.

"Birthdays must be big events for you," he said, drawing her from her musing.

"They should always be special."

He turned toward her, his knee brushing her leg, warming her with his touch. "Why's that?"

She wondered how to answer. She usually kept her memories close to the vest, but Dan had been forthcoming with her the other night when he'd told her about his childhood, about his sister.

"My grandmother planned my first and only party when I was eight. And it made me feel so...loved, so special. I'd known other kids who'd had celebrations each year, but they seemed more interested in the gifts they were going to receive."

"And you weren't?"

"Being treated like a princess was the best gift of all. And I made up my mind to make birthdays special when I had a family of my own."

She realized that she couldn't claim Dan's family as hers, but while she was here, she'd pretend that they were and treat them as such.

"You mentioned before that your childhood wasn't happy, but it sounds as though you had a nice grandmother and some good memories."

"My *abuelita* was a wonderful, loving woman, and she and I were really close. If she would have lived, I think my life would have turned out much differently." Eva had no doubt she would have been loved, happy, more balanced.

"What happened to her?"

"She had heart trouble, and she died right before my ninth birthday."

"I'm sorry."

"Me, too." Eva glanced at the moon, at the twinkling stars, then back at the man seated beside her. Their knees were still touching, fused together, it seemed.

"You know," she said, "it was good for me in a way."

"Losing your grandmother? I don't see how."

"She told me that I was smart, that I would be something special someday. And whenever my stepfather would belittle me, whenever he'd tell me I was stupid, I'd remember her and what she told me. And it taught me to be independent and self-sufficient. I worked extra-hard in school and earned a scholarship to Baylor University. And when I left home, I never looked back."

"I'm glad you escaped your stepfather, but I'm sorry you had to go through all of that."

"It was tough, but I learned to avoid him, especially when he'd been drinking." The scar on her neck tingled, as it sometimes did whenever she thought of the man's temper, his brutality.

Dan reached over and placed a hand on her knee. She expected a little pat, a gentle gesture. Yet he continued to touch her, and she was so glad that he did.

She felt an urge to lean into him, but she managed

to look straight ahead, beyond the ranch, beyond the moon and stars. Beyond an incredible sense of belonging to the universe, to the land, to the handsome cowboy beside her.

"This is new for me," Dan said.

Her heart soared, and hope fluttered in her chest. Was he talking about her? About *them?* About his feelings?

She both hoped and feared that he was.

"What's new?" she asked, holding her breath and waiting for him to steer the conversation into uncharted emotional territory.

"I rarely take the time to appreciate nights like this."

In a sense, Eva hadn't, either. But this evening, Dan's presence made it all the more special.

Still, the words she'd hoped to hear, the emotion she'd hoped he would express, never came. And then he'd given her that gentle pat on the knee she'd been expecting before he removed his hand completely.

She knew people made wishes on falling stars. And while she doubted that the moon held the same magic, she couldn't help closing her eyes and wishing that the sense of family and belonging that she'd experienced while on the Walker ranch would last forever.

Chapter Eight

As Eva's first few days on the ranch turned into a week, it became clear to Dan that everyone had taken a real shine to her—and not just Kaylee and Kevin.

Uncle Hank had really softened around the edges, especially at dinnertime. But he'd been more polite all the way around, more optimistic than before, more talkative.

On the other hand, Dan had tried hard to avoid Eva whenever he could. Yet, for some reason, he found himself seeking her out whenever the kids had turned in for the night.

It had all started after dinner last Saturday, when they'd spent an hour or so stargazing—and breathing in each other's scents. He wasn't sure if it was the shampoo she used or her perfume, but he couldn't seem to get enough of it.

In fact, if Kevin hadn't come outside to interrupt

them, Dan had no idea how long he would have continued to enjoy her company, her orange blossom fragrance, her...feminine essence.

Then the next night, they'd watched a chick flick after the kids and Hank had turned in. Dan knew he should have excused himself and found something else to do instead, but...well, heck. The movie was actually entertaining.

On Monday they'd played gin rummy in the den. She'd said she was a beginner, but she was sharp and had caught on quickly. She also had a competitive streak he hadn't expected. And for the first time in as long as he could remember, he'd had fun playing cards without a small wager on the table to make the game more interesting.

Each evening they'd done something different, something unexpected. In fact, yesterday after dinner, she'd been cutting big pink hearts out of construction paper. He'd asked what she was doing, and she'd explained that she'd planned some kind of craft project with the kids the next day.

Before he knew it, he was seated alongside her with a pair of scissors and cutting out a couple of big gold stars.

Tonight, they'd managed to go their separate ways, thanks to some bookwork he needed to take care of in the office. But when he finished, he decided to raid the cookie jar in the kitchen, only to find the light on and to see that she'd beat him to it.

She was wearing a blue robe over her white cotton nightgown. Her hair was loose—long and flowing—and her feet were bare, her toenails painted with pink polish.

Barefoot and pregnant came to mind. And he was... enchanted.

"Looks like we had the same idea," he said, "a bedtime snack."

She laughed. "I have to admit, I have a sweet tooth. Did you come for milk and cookies, too?"

That had been his game plan, but when he'd spotted her, he'd forgotten all about his love of chocolate, all about his decision to avoid her.

"Are there any left?"

She smiled and nodded. "I tripled the recipe. Between Hank and the kids, I can't seem to keep the cookie jar filled."

Earlier today he'd slipped off with a couple himself, but he didn't see any reason to confess.

Eva took several cookies from the jar and placed them on a saucer. Then she reached for two glasses from the cupboard and filled them with milk. Apparently, she figured they'd have their bedtime snack together, and he couldn't see any reason to object.

He watched as she completed the simple, domestic task. Something stirred deep inside of him as she stood there in her nightclothes, all soft and feminine and ready for bed.

"I've been thinking about the birthday celebration we're having for Hank," she said, leaning against the counter and making no move toward the table and chairs.

At that, he shook off thoughts of wrapping his arms around her soft body and tried to focus on their conversation. "What about it?"

"I know we're keeping it small, but I'd like to invite my friend Clara. Would you mind?"

"Of course, not. But I'm not sure what Hank will say to that. And when he gets his dander up, he can get pretty cranky."

"He's been so sweet lately." She reached for a chocolate chip cookie and broke it in half. "Do you think he'd really be upset about Clara coming?"

"I have no idea." His uncle might not want to see his life complicated any more than it already was. And Dan, more than anyone, could understand that. "But I think that some old flames were meant to burn out."

"I'm not trying to set them up. It's just that they used to be friends. And it might do them both good." She bit into the cookie—or rather, the jagged half she'd torn off. When she'd swallowed her first bite, she added, "I'd ask Clara first, and she might decline."

He supposed they wouldn't have to give any thought to Hank's possible reactions unless Clara actually accepted the invitation. And why would she? She'd obviously decided to marry another man for a reason, so he said, "Sure, why not?"

Eva seemed to ponder that for a while, or maybe she was just rehashing her plans for the party. Either way, he found himself watching her nibble at her bottom lip and wondering why such a simple movement could be so intriguing.

Finally, she looked up and said, "Even if Clara doesn't want to come, I'm going to ask for her chocolate cake recipe. You can't believe how good it is. I'm sure Hank will really like it."

Dan couldn't help smiling, couldn't help admiring the way Eva's brown eyes lit up—even if he wasn't so sure how his uncle would take to all the birthday fuss.

"I'm going to let the kids make the decorations," she added. "And we'll need to go shopping so they can pick out a gift for him."

"So much for having a little party." Dan realized he ought to object, but he didn't have the heart to disappoint her. "It sounds as though you're going all out."

"I just want the day to be special, that's all. And by remembering Hank and putting him first on the tenth of September, the kids will learn to think of others. That's important."

She was right, of course—as usual. He had to admit that he'd lost count of how many times he'd thanked his lucky stars that she'd come to help him. She was picking up the parental slack that he couldn't quite master.

Needless to say, his niece and nephew were much happier with Eva on the ranch. And if truth be told, so was he. As long as she was looking out for Kaylee and Kevin, he was not only able to focus on all the various chores that needed to be done, but he could rest assured that the kids were healthy, safe and happy.

"You know," he said, leaning his hip against the kitchen counter and reaching for a cookie of his own. "Kevin and Kaylee really like you. You're making a difference in their lives."

"Thanks. But they're not the only ones benefiting from all of this."

No, they weren't. And he wondered if Eva was picking up on the fact that Dan also liked her. That he was benefiting from her presence. That she might even be making a difference in his life, too.

"They're great kids," she said. "And I've grown close to them."

"I'm not surprised. You're a natural mother."

Her eyes brightened, and her cheeks flushed a pretty shade of pink. She lifted her hand to her chest and fingered the lace of her white cotton gown. The scar she often hid wasn't covered now, but it wasn't her flaws he was seeing. It was her beauty, her nurturing spirit, her generosity…

"Thank you so much for saying that," she said. "I've been worried about the kind of mom I'll be."

"You'll be the *best*. There's no doubt in my mind."

They stood just an arm's distance from each other, and while he probably should have suggested they carry their milk and cookies to the table—or better yet, take their bedtime snack back to their respective rooms—he didn't utter a word.

A wave of desire washed over him, and he was sorely tempted to reach out and touch her, to run his knuckles along her cheek.

As if she was suddenly aware of the push/pull that was going on inside of him, she tore her gaze from his and popped the rest of the cookie in her mouth, leaving a small crumb on her bottom lip.

Small? Actually, it was so miniscule that it really wouldn't be noticeable to anyone not studying the curve of her lips, the stretch of her smile.

Still, he brushed his thumb against her mouth, and her lips parted—half in surprise and half in arousal. But she wasn't the only one whose thoughts had taken a sexual turn.

He wanted to kiss her again in the worst way. And in her eyes, he could see that she wanted it, too.

But that wasn't a good idea. As a result, he tried to call upon his better judgment, his common sense, but it was a losing battle.

Aw, hell. Who was he kidding? The desire to take her in his arms and let nature run its course had gone amok, and there was no stopping it now.

He took a single step closer, slipped his arms around her waist and drew her close. He supposed he could still backpedal if he wanted to, but the light citrus scent of her shampoo, the warmth of her embrace, sent his pulse reeling and his better judgment tumbling by the wayside.

As he lowered his mouth to hers, he wasn't sure what he was getting into, but it didn't matter right now. He might be able to come up with a hundred reasons to stop, but he'd never felt such a rush, such a desire to kiss a woman before.

Sure, he'd had lovers in the past—*plenty* of them. He was thirty-eight years old and as male as they came. But none of them had ever gotten under his skin before, not like this, not like Eva.

As hands roamed and hearts pounded, the kiss deepened. Their breaths mingled and their tongues mated. Her taste—as sweet as sugar and laced with chocolate—damn near sent him over the edge. He couldn't seem to get enough, and he wanted to take her right here and right now.

But no way could he do that with a house full of people. And as he thought about taking her to bed—he didn't care whose—he realized his folly.

He had to get control of his senses, and as he forced himself to do so, he finally pulled back and broke the kiss.

She swayed slightly, then reached for his shoulder to steady herself, clearly as aroused as he was.

What would she say if he suggested that they take this kiss into the privacy of his bedroom?

It didn't matter what she said, he realized. He couldn't do that. It was all too much, too fast. Too soon.

As he drew away, he wanted to say something clever, to laugh it off. But he couldn't come up with anything but an apology that he practically stumbled over.

"You don't have anything to be sorry about," she said.

The hell he didn't. He was sorry that things were complicated, that they both had more baggage than they knew what to do with. That he'd been entrusted with two kids too many—sweet as they were. And as attracted as he was becoming to Eva, Kaylee and Kevin had to come first.

How could he take on any more than that? And getting involved with Eva would mean that he'd have to give up life as he knew it.

So he offered her a half-assed smile and said, "I guess it's been a long time since I've had a beautiful woman in my kitchen during the witching hour."

Okay, so it wasn't anywhere near midnight, but that didn't mean there wasn't some bewitching going on. And for a man who'd never intended to marry and have children, he really ought to get the hell out of Dodge before he did or said something stupid that would lead her to believe differently.

So he ran his knuckles along her cheek, told her to sleep tight, then turned and headed for the door.

"You forgot your cookies," she said.

That wasn't all he'd forgotten. He'd been so caught up in that blood-stirring kiss that he'd forgotten who he was, who she was.

Still, he returned to the counter, reached for the stack on the saucer and snatched a couple of cookies to take with him, although he wasn't sure why he did. The taste of chocolate from her lips had satisfied his sweet tooth.

Too bad it hadn't done a damn thing to douse his libido, which, at this very minute, was chomping at the bit for more.

It had taken Dan forever to fall asleep last night. That intoxicating kiss he'd shared with Eva kept replaying in his mind, and he'd kicked himself until the wee hours of the morning.

What had gotten into him? He'd been so determined to keep things platonic with her, but whenever he was anywhere near her, it seemed that his best intentions went up in smoke.

On both occasions when he'd let down his guard and kissed her, the sexual sparks had gone off in his head like the Fourth of July, and his hormones had soared as if there were no tomorrow.

What a mess he'd made of things—and he had another week of temptation.

He'd finally rolled out of bed just before dawn, showered and dressed for the day. Then, while everyone was still sleeping, he went into the kitchen and put on a pot of coffee, adding extra grounds to make sure it was strong and infused with caffeine.

The water sputtered, the pot roared to life and, before long, the heady aroma of the fresh morning brew filled the room.

Jack, who had a bed on the service porch, had been sleeping with the kids these days. He usually came trotting into the kitchen as soon as he knew someone was up. But he'd been a little slow this morning.

"Hey," Dan said, when the cattle dog finally moseyed through the door. "Are you hungry, boy?"

Jack wagged his tail, then headed for his bowl, knowing what was next.

Dan fed him and checked his water, then he returned to the kitchen. He poured himself a mug and reached into the cookie jar for a little breakfast-on-the-run. Trouble was, when he took a bite, the taste of brown sugar, vanilla and chocolate reminded him of Eva, of the sweet taste of her kiss last night, and he swore under his breath.

Was he ever going to kick the memory of her embrace or the growing desire to take her to bed?

He had at least five or six days of temptation to go, and it wasn't going to be easy. He glanced at his wristwatch, realizing Manuel would be arriving soon.

Good. A diversion.

He left the house, crossed the yard, entered the barn and turned on the light switch. One of several bulbs went out, letting him know it was time to replace them.

Jill, who'd been snoozing with her pups in a bed of straw, yawned and stretched. Then she left her squirming babies and came to greet him, tail wagging.

"It's chow time, Mama." He gave the dog a good rub behind the ears, then went to get her a bowl of food and some fresh water.

Next he checked the mare and her filly, who were doing just fine.

Filly, puppies, kids...

The ranch had become a nursery, it seemed. Who would have guessed?

Dan kept himself busy for the next hour or so, then he returned to the kitchen, refilled his mug and grabbed a quick breakfast: a couple more cookies and a banana.

He was just about to slip outside again when Hank entered the room and made his way to the cupboard, where he pulled out a white mug.

"You're up early," the old man said, as he poured himself a cup of the morning brew.

"I've got a lot to do." Dan figured it was a better answer than the truth—that he hadn't slept worth a damn after kissing Eva.

"Hey," Kevin said from the doorway. "What's going on in here?"

"Nothing. Breakfast won't be ready for a while. Why don't you go on back to bed?"

"I can't. Jack licked my face until he woke me up." The boy rubbed his eyes and scanned the room. "Where's Eva?"

Dan had no idea, although he suspected she'd be coming soon. "Are you hungry? I can give you something to tide you over."

When the boy nodded, Dan handed him a cookie.

"Cool." Kevin brightened. "I like it when *you* fix breakfast, Uncle Dan. You know what guys would rather eat."

He chuckled. "Yeah, well, that's not the real thing. It's just a snack."

Kevin took his cookie and joined Jack on the service porch. Moments later, the back door squeaked open, and the pajama-clad kid and the dog went outside.

When a vehicle sounded, Dan glanced out the window.

"That must be Manuel," Hank said.

He was right. Dan dumped the remainder of his coffee in the sink, then rinsed the mug. "I'd better go outside and line him up for the day."

As he made his way through the door, he had to step around Kevin, who was seated smack dab in the middle of the steps, munching on the chocolate chip cookie and petting Jack.

"Where are you going, Uncle Dan?"

"I've got to talk to Manuel, then I'm going to fix the corral gate. The hinge is busted."

"Can I help you?"

"I appreciate the offer, sport. But I can't think of anything you can do to help right now."

"I'm pretty strong." He lifted his right arm and flexed. "Want to see my muscle?"

At times, Dan spotted something that reminded him of Jenny when he looked at her kids—an expression, the way they cocked their heads, something in their eyes—and he couldn't help but smile.

As much as the twins had put a cramp in his life and increased his stress and worry tenfold, he actually liked having them around. There was something about them that tugged at his heart, something that made him want to do whatever he could to keep them safe and to make them happy.

So he walked over to Kevin, felt the scrawny little arm and made a big deal over the biceps muscles that wouldn't develop for years. "Well, I'll be darned. Will you look at that? You certainly *are* strong. I'll keep that in mind."

Dan made his way across the yard to Manuel, who was just climbing out of his pickup.

"There's a good size stretch of fence along the county road that needs some repair work," Manuel said. "I spotted it on my way here this morning."

"Does it need to be replaced?"

"I think we can get by without any major expense, but it'll take some time and some work."

While the men talked, Kevin and Jack strode into the barn, probably with the intention of checking on the puppies. The boy was barefoot and wearing pajamas, so Dan would have to tell him to get dressed and put on his shoes after he talked to Manual.

"I'll saddle a horse and check it out closer," he told the hand. "Then I'll figure out what we'll need from the hardware store."

"You want me to ride with you, boss?"

"That's not necessary. I can do it."

A thump sounded, followed by a wail that could only have been made by an injured child.

Dan cursed under his breath as he dashed into the barn. When he spotted Kevin laying on the ground near the stall gate and sobbing, anger and frustration slammed into him.

"What in the hell did you do now?" he snapped, his voice coming out a lot harsher than he'd meant it to.

The boy wailed as he got to his knees. He removed his hand from his mouth, which was full of blood. When he saw it, he cried even louder.

Damn. What had he done? Dan's heart pounded like a son of a gun as he searched the boy's face for damage.

Oh, for cripe's sake. He'd knocked out his front teeth.

"Did you have a loose tooth before?" Dan asked.

The boy shook his head no. "Why?"

Dan wasn't sure what to tell him. Just seeing the blood had shaken Kevin to the core. How was he going to react when he realized the extent of his injury?

The boy wailed again, and Dan felt like crap. Not a day went by that something didn't happen to one of the kids. And this time Dan had clearly slipped up and dropped the ball.

"I've got some good news for you," Dan said, trying to take Eva's usual tack.

"Wh-aaat's that?" Kevin sobbed, the blood dribbling down his chin and dripping to the ground.

"You get to put your teeth under your pillow tonight, and in the morning, you'll be rich."

"A *tooth* came out of my mouth?" the boy shrieked.

"It looks like two of them did."

"Oh, no!"

Dan had no idea how bad Kevin's injury was, but his mouth was really bleeding. He hated to see the kid upset and wondered what Eva would have said to him had she been here instead of Dan.

Of course, if she were, she wouldn't have let this happen.

"I'd say you're pretty lucky," Dan lied. "You're going to have a visit from the Tooth Fairy."

Dan had never had any experience with the typical childhood fantasy heroes like Santa, the Easter Bunny or the Tooth Fairy. So he wasn't entirely sure how it was supposed to work. And even if he was able to fake it, he had no idea what the going rate was for teeth these days. But the upset and trauma alone made him want to make it worth the kid's time.

Yet even though he would be able to peel off a twenty from his money clip and tuck it under the boy's pillow tonight, that wasn't going to make up for his failings as a parent.

An hour after Eva cleaned up Kevin's mouth and determined he didn't need medical attention—at least not *this* time—Dan didn't feel the least bit better about his nephew's injury.

Sure, it tore him up to see the little guy hurt and bleeding. And if he could have traded places and taken on the pain himself, he would have done it in a heartbeat—even if it meant losing two permanent teeth. How did real parents deal with this sort of thing?

But worse than that was the guilt and the realization that he should have been watching the kids closer.

If he didn't know better, he'd swear that there was a gray rain cloud following him around ever since the kids had come to stay on the ranch. He couldn't seem to do anything right, even if his heart was in the right place.

Failure never had set very well with him. Neither had fear. And when it came to the kids, he knew that it was only a matter of time before he crashed and burned.

The telephone rang, and Dan welcomed the interruption. But when he answered, he snapped at the caller a bit more than he'd meant to. "Hello?"

"Hi, Dan."

He didn't recognize the woman's voice right off. "Who is this?"

"It's Catherine. I called to check on the kids. I really miss them."

How badly did she miss them? Bad enough to want them to return to New York? To stay with her again? Was that the reason for her call?

He had guardianship. That meant he could make decisions based upon what would be best for the kids. But he and Catherine had already gone over that. She had a part in a big show, which kept her out late at night. And her days were full of rehearsals, so the kids would be stuck with a babysitter day in and day out. A pang of guilt stabbed him for even considering it, though deep down he felt even a babysitter might make a better parent then him.

"Are they doing okay?" she asked, drawing him back into the conversation.

Relatively speaking. At least they hadn't been seriously injured yet. But who knew what tomorrow would bring?

"They're doing fine," he said, keeping news of the stitches and the missing teeth to himself. "How about you?"

"I'm all right. Are the kids settling in? Are you feeling better about taking care of them?"

It depended, he supposed. Kaylee and Kevin might be getting the hang of ranch life, but he wasn't cut out for fatherhood. Did he dare tell his sister's old roommate that Kaylee had visited the E.R. last week and had her wound glued shut? Or that Kevin had gotten a knot on his head the other day and had knocked out his front teeth today?

"It's all right," he said, "but I'm not much of a father figure."

"I'm sure you're doing fine."

Yeah, well, he didn't know about that. Yet he wasn't about to admit it.

"I've been thinking about the kids lately," she added. "I had no idea how quiet the apartment would be without them here."

"I'm sure they miss you, too. How's the play going?"

"I'm afraid my run on Broadway ended a couple of days ago."

"What happened?"

She blew out a wobbly sigh. "I fell during practice and broke my arm."

He knew how badly she'd wanted that part. "I'm sorry to hear that, Catherine."

"Me, too. But that's the way it goes."

He supposed she was right. Life was full of disappointments, and people just had to deal with them and go on. "So what are you doing now?"

"Not much."

Did that mean she had time to spend with the kids again?

Did he dare ask? It would certainly be better if taking Kaylee and Kevin was her idea. It was bad enough having people learn he was a parental failure, but even worse to have them think he was just trying to get rid of the kids.

It might seem that way, he supposed. But either way—keeping them or letting them go—were both unsettling options. And there was no way for him to come out on top.

As silence stretched across the line, a lightbulb went on in his head and an idea formed—wild as it was.

"How would you like it if they came for a visit?" he asked.

"Here? To New York? Are you kidding?"

No. He was as serious as a toothless grin, a knot on the noggin and a scar across a little girl's brow. "Not at all. I'd been thinking about surprising you."

"Wow. That would be great."

"How about this weekend?" he asked.

"It's Thursday already. You aren't talking about to-morrow, are you?"

"If I can get a flight for us." He had a slew of airline miles that had accrued over the past year, credits that would be lost if he didn't use them one of these days. So why not? "I'll give you a call later and let you know if I can pull it off."

"I'd love to see them," she said. "I've missed them even more than I imagined."

"I'm sure you have."

"It's hard to explain. I know they're not mine, but I spent so much time with them it sure feels as though they are."

Dan was glad to hear it. And he could understand what she meant. He'd certainly grown attached to the kids in the short time he'd had them. Maybe that's why it made him so uneasy to be in complete charge of them, so afraid that he'd fail them sooner or later—and in a way that was far worse than a bump or a bruise.

When the line disconnected, he stared at the telephone receiver in his hand for the longest time before finally hanging up.

He hadn't been entirely truthful with Catherine. He'd mentioned taking the kids to New York for a visit. But what he hadn't said was that he planned to ask her to take them again—permanently. If they saw each other face-to-face, he had a feeling they'd all agree.

And as sure as he was that he was making the right decision for everyone involved, something tightened in his chest, and he couldn't help feeling as though he was losing his sister all over again.

Chapter Nine

When Dan broke the news about going to New York to the kids, you'd have thought that he'd just announced that tomorrow was Christmas Eve.

"We get to visit Catherine?" Kevin brightened, his missing front teeth making him look a couple years older than he really was.

"And we get to see our friends, Jimmy and Carly?" Kaylee asked.

See? He'd been right. The kids *were* missing their lives in New York.

"We haven't seen them in a long time," Kevin said.

Dan studied the children's expressions, trying to determine if his speculation was right. "You miss Catherine, don't you?"

"I miss Mommy more," Kaylee said, sadness creeping into her voice.

Her brother dropped his head. "Me, too."

Dan hadn't wanted to remind them of their loss. But if truth be told, he'd lost Jenny, their mommy, too. His grief, though, had kicked in the day she'd left the ranch seeking a life he couldn't understand.

He'd gotten over it, of course, and had learned to live without his sister, who'd been the only family he'd ever had. He'd grown to manhood and had learned to emulate Hank, who'd taught him how to ranch, how to cowboy.

But no one had taught him how to parent, how to father. He glanced at Kaylee, with the fading pink scar that stretched across her forehead, and then at Kevin, with his jack-o'-lantern smile.

Raising kids was a huge responsibility, one he'd taken on and would take on again and again—but not if there was a better option.

And Catherine was that option.

"When are we going to New York?" Kevin asked.

"I found a flight that leaves late this afternoon," Dan said.

"*Today?* We get to go *now?*" Kaylee brightened, then ran to Dan and gave him a hug.

Her brother followed suit, and their burst of happiness, their enthusiastic response, turned Dan inside out.

As Eva entered the room, both children turned to her and smiled. "Uncle Dan is going to take us to New York to see Catherine."

"That's great." She smiled, and Dan realized her enthusiasm had an effect on him, too.

"Can Eva go to New York with us?" Kaylee asked.

Are you crazy, Dan wanted to ask the kid. A huge

part of this whole plan was finding a way for him to avoid her, too. A way to save his sorry butt from the rush of unwelcome attraction he felt whenever she entered the room.

But no one knew what was going on in his mind, and he planned to keep it that way.

"When are you leaving?" Eva asked the children, as she swept into the kitchen and opened the refrigerator door.

"Today!" Kaylee's excitement was impossible to ignore, and Dan again realized he was doing the right thing—even if letting them go and knowing they were so happy about it left him a little uneasy, a little unbalanced.

Eva nearly dropped the jug of milk she'd been taking out of the fridge. With the door still wide-open, she turned to Dan, her gaze seeking his for confirmation, for an explanation. *"Today?"*

"I know it's a little quick, but the opportunity came up suddenly, and I took advantage of it." He offered her a no-big-deal grin. "I have some airline miles that are going to expire at the end of the month, so I figured I'd better use them."

Okay, so that part hadn't been entirely true. They were good until the end of this year. A guilty weight, the size of an anvil dropped into his gut. He hated to lie to her—or to anyone—but he'd started the ball rolling this morning, after Catherine's call, and he couldn't very well stop it at this point.

Besides, how did he tell her that he was orchestrating a change in custody?

He had to admit that it wasn't going to be easy to give up the kids. But it wasn't just their smiles and excitement that he found contagious. Their tears and disappointments knocked a hard wallop, too. When they hurt, he hurt. And those shared emotions were about to do him in.

Over the years, Dan had become adept at resisting and avoiding anything at which he might fail. And the ploy had worked well for him.

The first time he'd been thrown from a horse, he'd gotten back on and had done his best to get the hang of roping and riding.

But the emotional stuff that Kaylee and Kevin inadvertently threw his way on an hourly basis was a lot tougher to master, and he wasn't sure he even wanted to try. Not any longer. Not when there was a viable option in New York.

Dan glanced across the kitchen at Eva and saw her watching him. She'd already closed the fridge, but she still held the milk—her movements frozen, it seemed.

Her expression was intense, the thoughts in her mind clearly churning. The news had apparently thrown her for a loop.

"I've got enough miles for Eva to go with us," he finally said in answer to Kaylee's question, "but she probably isn't up for a quick trip like that. This is pretty short notice."

"But if she *wants* to go with us," Kaylee said, "she can go, too, can't she?"

"Sure," Dan said, figuring Eva would probably decline. After all, it was such short notice, and they wouldn't stay very long. But when he tossed a glance her way, when he saw those cogs and wheels turning

in her mind, when he saw the glimmer in those intoxicating brown eyes grow bright, he wasn't sure about
anything anymore.

Eva stood in the center of the kitchen, flabbergasted
by the conversation taking place. She'd come in to pour
herself a glass of milk and to put on a pot of soup
for lunch, but she was no longer hungry, no longer
thirsty.

What was up with a sudden trip to New York? Dan
had brought it up as though it was nothing more than
a Sunday stroll in the park.

Eva hated to see the kids go, even for a weekend
visit, which was strange—and not the least bit logical.
After all, they weren't her children. But she'd become
attached to them during her stay at the ranch and wasn't
ready to see it end. And as much as she hated to admit
it, she'd been playing house the past couple of days and
wasn't ready to go back to her own empty house and
quiet life.

She wouldn't try to understand it, though. She'd been
dealing with logic for so long, the emotional aspects of
life were difficult for her to deal with, to comprehend
or to trust.

"Please," Kaylee begged. "Go with us to New York,
Eva."

It was then that Eva realized she hadn't responded
yet, that she'd been so unbalanced by Dan's announce-
ment, that she didn't know what to say.

"Yeah," Kevin said. "Go with us. You can see Catherine and Jimmy and Carly."

"Please," Kaylee begged again, and something

warm and wobbly rose up in Eva. Something soft and pressing.

Eva glanced at her wristwatch, although she wasn't sure why. Then she turned to Dan. "What time does the flight leave?"

He blinked, and his expression morphed into something stiff and completely unreadable. "Three o'clock."

"Out of Houston?"

He nodded.

"That means we'd have to pack and leave here by…?" The wristwatch came in handy now, as she tried to determine how much time she had to pack.

"Within the next hour," Dan said.

"You can be ready," Kaylee said. "Me and Kevin can help you."

The child's innocence, the hope-filled eyes, the emotion on her sweet face turned Eva every which way but loose, and a flood of what could only be described as maternal warmth washed over her.

It had to be her hormones at work.

Nevertheless, she couldn't say no. "All right. I'll go, too—assuming your uncle can get the ticket for me and that he doesn't mind if I tag along."

The kids let out a happy cheer, but when she glanced at Dan, his expression, while having grown softer, wasn't anywhere near as easy to read.

The flight to New York was uneventful, other than Kevin setting off the metal detector with a pocket full of Matchbox cars. But eventually, they got through security and boarded a 320 Airbus and settled into their seats.

They took off about ten minutes early, but with the time change, they still arrived too late into La Guardia to go straight to Catherine's place. So Dan hailed a cab and had it take them to a hotel in midtown, where he'd stayed the last time he was here.

He glanced at Eva, trying to gauge how she was doing. But as she craned her neck and studied sights, he decided she was curious, intrigued.

The kids, while sleepy, had perked up and had begun to chatter about this thing and that—about people they knew, places they'd been. It was clear that they'd come home to where they were comfortable, where life was as it should be.

Minus their mother, of course.

The cabbie dropped them off in front of the hotel. After Dan paid and tipped the driver, he herded his little entourage into the lobby.

He'd been so busy buying airline tickets, making arrangements and packing, that he hadn't given the sleeping accommodations much thought on the trip over, although he didn't know why he hadn't. The four of them couldn't very well stay in one room.

"We're going to need two rooms," he told the clerk at the reservation desk. "But can you make them adjoining?"

"I'm sorry, we're nearly full tonight. It's a weekend, and without calling ahead for reservations... You'll be lucky if I can find one room. Let me see what I can do."

Dan wasn't sure what he'd do if they couldn't find accommodations. If this hotel was full, others would be, too.

"I don't mind sharing a room," Eva said. "As long

as there are two beds, I can sleep with Kaylee, and you can sleep with Kevin. It's only one night."

She was right, but for some crazy reason, he'd prefer to bunk with Eva, rather than one of the kids.

How was that for getting soft? And stupid?

"I do have one option that might work," the clerk said as he tapped away on a computer. "How about a minisuite? It has two doubles and a separate living area with a small refrigerator. Would that work?"

It would have to.

Several minutes later, they were given plastic card keys and sent up to the tenth floor. The kids were thrilled with the accommodations, and Dan supposed it was going to be fine. He just hadn't expected them all to pile into one room.

But, hey. It wasn't that big of a deal. They shared a house, which was just a little bit larger.

Eva took over from there, getting the kids in the bath, then helping them put on the pajamas. And he went down to the corner deli and purchased sandwiches to go. Tomorrow, after he'd delivered the kids to Catherine, he could show Eva around—not that he was any expert.

It was funny, though. As long as the kids weren't in the picture, the idea of anything remotely datelike with Eva didn't bother him as much as he would have guessed.

He supposed it was the family thing that worried him the most, the responsibility of looking out for someone else, of taking care of their emotional needs and making sure they were happy. The need to assume a role he wasn't equipped to take on.

When he returned with turkey sandwiches, chips and

brownies for dessert, Eva and the children were ready for bed. But it wasn't the kids who caught his eye when he let himself into the room. It was the lovely woman dressed in a white cotton gown, with her glossy hair hanging down her back.

It was hard not to stare, not to comment about her beauty, her innocence. Even with the slight bulge of her pregnancy, there was something that appealed to him on a sexual level. And as she laughed about something Kaylee had said, he realized that she had a maternal streak a mile long, even if she didn't know it.

The kids ate only a little of what he'd brought them, and when they'd finished, Eva tucked each one of them in bed.

For a moment, Dan wished that they were a real family, that the kids could double up together, and that he and Eva could slip between the covers....

But they couldn't. A family of four was one thing. But a family of six?

That would be emotional suicide for Dan. And wasn't that why he was here? To make sure the kids were cared for, that their needs were all met? That they'd be safe? That they'd grow up happy?

Still, that didn't mean he wasn't powerfully attracted to Eva.

"Come on," he said. "Let's sit on the sofa and watch a little television."

She agreed, then cleared the table. As she did so, he raided the minibar in the fridge and carried their drinks—a beer for him and a juice for her—into the living area of the small hotel room. But he didn't turn on the TV.

For some reason, he wanted to just be near her, to talk to her.

As she sat beside him on the small sofa, nearly close enough to touch, he said, "You don't look like a scientist tonight."

She turned to him, her knee nudging his. But she seemed oblivious to the fact they were touching, to the warmth that was rushing from her to him.

"I'm sorry," she said, her brow furrowed. "I should have brought a robe. I didn't think…"

That they'd end up sharing a room? It's not like they didn't have built-in chaperones, although, when he glanced across the room, he saw that they'd both dozed off.

"Don't worry about that." A smile stretched across his lips. "You look great, Eva—whether you have a robe or not. I was just making a comment."

And it had been a compliment, although he wasn't sure if he should pursue it. Not with their legs touching, his blood warming and his hormones pumping.

"Thank you." Her hand lifted, and she fingered the taut, darkened scar tissue that stretched along her throat and behind the lace neckline of her gown.

"Does it hurt?" he asked.

Her fingers stopped, froze. Then they trailed along her neck, along the length of the scar—at least the part he could see. "You mean, this?"

He nodded.

"No, it doesn't hurt anymore."

"What happened?" He shouldn't have asked. And he hadn't intended to. For a guy who liked to keep his past to himself, he didn't usually pry into other people's lives.

She paused for the longest time, and when he was about to apologize and tell her that it didn't matter, that it wasn't any of his business, she said, "My stepfather had a temper."

Dan's stomach clenched. She'd told him enough for him to know that her past had been painful. And while he'd had firsthand experience with neglect, he'd never had to deal with physical abuse. Not like that.

"One day," she explained, "when I was about twelve, the bathroom sink was clogged. He accused me of causing the problem, although I have no idea what I might have done."

Dan wanted to reach over, to take her hand, to tell her she didn't need to go on, that he got the picture. But he let her talk, thinking it might be good if she did.

"He wasn't having much luck in fixing it. And in his anger and frustration, he threw the drain cleaner at me."

Dan grimaced. "I'm sorry."

She shrugged. "It could have been worse. It missed my face and my eyes."

In a sense, she was right. But the fact that a parent—step or otherwise—would be so angry, would be so cruel, so thoughtless, turned his stomach.

"I do my best to cover it up, but not because I'm self-conscious. It's just that I try hard to forget what happened in the past. And when I look at it or when someone asks me about it...well, the memory is front and center again."

"I'm sorry. I shouldn't have brought it up."

"That's okay." She smiled, reached over and gave his hand a pat. "In a sense, it was a good thing that it happened. My teacher reported it, social workers removed me from the house and I made up my mind to do something with my life, to use my academic skills and get a college degree. That led to a medical career and a life of my own making."

Still, it was a shame she had to go through what she had. It wasn't fair. Kids were supposed to be loved, protected.

She glanced down, but not at anything in particular, and he caught a sense of sadness, loneliness—even if she had come out on top over the years.

Was that why she'd chosen to have in vitro fertilization? Had she steered clear of male relationships because of the guy who'd abused her? He hoped that wasn't the case, because if it was, she carried more scars than the one on her neck.

"Did you have many friends when you were a kid?" Dan asked, hoping that she had some emotional support.

"Not many. I didn't want anyone to ever come home with me, to see how we lived." She smiled again, as if breaking free of the dark memories, as if shoving them aside. "I was also pretty quiet and embarrassed by the way I looked."

"The way you looked?" Didn't she realize how pretty she was? Or had she been an ugly duckling, a gangly little thing that hadn't grown into her full beauty yet?

"Money was hard to come by, so I got my clothes from the thrift store. Up until the time I went to college, I never quite developed a sense of style or the confidence to pull it off."

"You could have fooled me."

"What do you mean?"

"You need to take a good, long look in the mirror,

Eva. But first you'd better take off those blinders that jerk of a stepfather forced you to wear."

Blinders?

What was he suggesting? That she'd been unable to see herself clearly? That simply wasn't true, was it? Eva had taken plenty of good, hard looks at herself, at her abilities, at her contributions to the world.

Uneasy with his sympathy, if that's what it was, Eva shook off the past the best she could. "For the most part, I've done that. I got my degree in biology, went on to become a medical technologist and landed the lab position at the Brighton Valley Medical Center. And my life is finally coming together."

At least, it seemed to be coming together before she met Dan and the kids and had come to stay at the ranch for a while. They were providing a whole new dimension to her life, something she hadn't realized she'd been missing.

"Are you happy there?"

"Where?" she asked. "At the medical center?"

He nodded.

"Yes. I'm good at what I do. I help save lives—in my own way. And I like and admire my colleagues. The only thing missing in my life was having a family of my own. So I took the bull by the horns and had in vitro fertilization.

Life was brighter than it had ever been before, although she was still a little concerned about bringing home and caring for two newborns on her own.

But Kaylee and Kevin were having a real, ego-plumping effect on her, even though it was a struggle for her to second-guess them sometimes or to do the right thing.

So she had no doubt she'd make a good mother—with a little time and practice.

She looked over her shoulder at the sleeping children, who were dozing as if they didn't have a care in the world.

That was good, she decided.

"Do you want to use the bathroom first?" Dan asked.

"Sure." She got to her feet, then strode across the room to the carry-on bag in which she'd packed her things.

As she unzipped it and reached inside for her toiletries, she glanced out the window at the city lights and her breath caught.

"Look at that," she said, leaving her bag and walking closer to the window. "It's beautiful outside. Look at the lights, the activity."

But she didn't have to wait long for him to join her. His voice sounded right beside her. "My sister liked Manhattan, too."

She turned, facing him. "You don't?"

"I'd rather be in Texas. At the ranch."

"Then why'd you come? You practically moved heaven and earth to bring the kids for a weekend visit."

He grew silent for a moment, as if the answer wasn't all that easy. "The kids were born and raised here. This is the world they know."

She had to agree; he was right. And as she looked down ten stories to the people rushing along the sidewalk below, she realized that kids adapted to all kinds of things.

They'd been happy on the ranch, at the airport, in

the cab. Too bad adults weren't quite as flexible when
it came to changes in their own lives.

"Kaylee and Kevin would be better off here," he
said, "in the city."

Better off than at the ranch? Eva couldn't see how.
And she wondered what he meant by that.

She turned away from the window, saw him leaning
against the sill, his breath fogging the glass, his head
bowed.

So he'd dropped everything and brought them for a
visit, even though he had a ranch to run.

Her heart skipped a beat as she realized the efforts
Dan would go to for his niece and nephew. And she
realized what a loving uncle he was.

She eased closer to him and placed her hand on his
shoulder. "You're a good man, Dan Walker."

He glanced up, his gaze snagging hers and dragging
her deep inside of him. "Am I?"

"Yes," she said, her voice coming out choked with
both admiration and emotion. "You're the best."

She placed a hand on his cheek, felt the bristle of
the beard he'd be shaving in the morning.

He placed his hand over hers, holding it to his face.
"Thanks. But I'm far from perfect."

He was, she realized, just as insecure as she was
about raising kids and being a parent. And at that moment, she felt herself falling for him—hook, line and
sinker.

Chapter Ten

The next morning, Dan woke to the sound of horns honking outside their hotel room, and he realized they were burning daylight.

Kevin had tossed and turned all night, and Dan had been forced to move to the very edge of the bed to avoid the kid's feet in his face or his ribs. Of course, knowing that Eva was sleeping just steps away from him hadn't helped.

Last night, when she'd reached out and touched him, when their eyes had met and locked, everything inside him had turned to mush, and he'd forgotten why they couldn't get involved.

Of course, without the kids in the equation, things might be different. At least, if she didn't expect him to be a part of her children's lives.

He hadn't exactly come out and told her why he'd brought them all to New York, but she was a bright woman. He suspected that she was able to read between the lines.

The kids belonged to the city, just as their mother apparently had. And he was country born and bred.

In the bed next to him, the sheets rustled. He rolled to the side and saw Eva looking across the room at him.

It had been weird sharing a room with her, yet not sharing a bed. And he wondered what it would be like to lie with her, to hold her through the night, to wake with her in his arms.

Of course, with the kids here, that was impossible.

Oddly enough, their presence made him refuse to consider getting involved with her. He wasn't a family kind of guy.

If Catherine agreed to take Kaylee and Kevin, would his feelings about an involvement with Eva change?

It depended, he supposed. As long as she didn't expect him to step in and be a father to her twins, it might.

"You hungry?" he asked, noting that one of the buttons on the neckline of her gown had come undone during the night, revealing the soft mound of one of her breasts.

"Yes," she said, as she stretched and yawned, "a little."

"There was a bakery right next to the deli that made our sandwiches last night. It looked like it had a large variety of things in their display case. Why don't I get something for us to eat there?"

"Good idea."

He threw off the covers, then paused as he realized he'd stripped down to his boxers last night.

She seemed to sense his reluctance to parade across the room in his shorts and rolled over toward the far wall. So he used the opportunity to grab a change of clothes and to slip into the bathroom. Then he took a quick shower and shaved.

When he came out, the kids were awake and the television was on.

"Can I go with you?" Kevin asked. "I'm already dressed."

The boy had on his shoes and socks and was wearing a pair of jeans and a blue T-shirt, but his hair stuck up on one side of his head.

But what the heck. Dan would water it down when they got back to the room. "Sure, you can go."

After telling Eva that they'd be back shortly, Dan took Kevin to the elevator and rode it to the lobby. Nodding at the doorman, he placed a hand on the boy's head and ushered him through the revolving doors and to the street.

"Where are we going?" Kevin asked. "Are we riding the subway?"

"We don't have to. The place we're looking for is just a block or two away."

Dan shoved his hands into the pockets of his jeans and they walked along the sidewalk, through several intersections and to the bakery he'd visited the last time he was in Manhattan.

He felt better about the place this time around, since he was getting a feel for the city, for the way the subway system ran.

As they walked, Kevin chattered up a storm, not the least bit intimidated by the mad rush of the city, by people who whizzed past him.

"Here it is," he said, as he turned into the little shop that smelled of fresh brewed coffee, sugar and spice.

At lunchtime, they offered killer sandwiches. But their sweet rolls were the best he'd ever tasted. If he actually lived in Manhattan, he'd make this a regular stop each morning.

But he couldn't imagine living here.

They made their way to the counter and waited their turn.

"I want that one," Kevin said, pointing at a tray in the display case. "The one with chocolate and whipped cream."

"I'm going to get you and Kaylee one of the ham-and-egg croissants to split. Then after you've had that, you can share one of the sweet rolls."

Kevin grumbled, clearly not happy about having protein first—or sharing with his sister.

"You sound like Eva," Kevin said. "She always makes us eat the good stuff last."

"Protein is better for you than sugar," Dan said. "All cowboys have to keep that in mind."

"Can I help you?" the clerk, a twentysomething brunette with her hair in a ponytail, asked.

"Yes. I'd like three of those ham-and-egg croissants—" Feeling a little more confident about knowing what to feed the kids—thanks to Eva—he added, "And a couple of fruit cups, three milks and a coffee." Then he ordered the chocolate éclair Kevin had picked out and a couple others that Eva could choose from.

The clerk tallied up the bill, which was pretty expensive, at least by Brighton Valley standards. But there was one thing Dan had learned about New York—no matter how much it cost, the food was usually pretty darn good.

He handed the girl a couple of twenties, and she made change. Then he picked up the sacks she'd packed to carry back to the hotel room.

"Come on Kev," he said. "Let's head back."

No answer.

Dan glanced to his right and to his left.

No kid.

The place was buzzing with activity, though—people moving in and out.

"Kevin!" he called.

No answer.

"Where's my kid?" he asked the clerk, who shrugged, then scanned the small shop. "I didn't see a kid with you."

Oh, for cripe's sake.

"Has anyone seen a little boy?" Dan asked, the panic rising in his voice. Where the heck could he be? He was just here a minute ago.

"Kevin!" he hollered again, wondering if it was too soon to call the police, to sound some kind of alarm.

God, what could have happened to him? Had someone snatched him? Kids got kidnapped all the time.

He tried to tell himself not to panic, not to worry. Kevin had a tendency to wander. But if they'd been in Brighton Valley, Dan might have felt better about him taking off. But here? In Manhattan?

Dan's gut twisted, and his heart dropped. What if something happened to Kevin? What if he got lost? What if someone snatched him?

Someone, a little someone, tapped on Dan's thigh, and he glanced down to see Kevin.

"Oh, my God." He didn't know if he should lash out at the kid for disappearing or break down and cry in relief that nothing horrible had happened to him. As it was, he did both.

"Where the hell did you go?" he blurted out, as he dropped to his knees and hugged the kid close.

"I had to go to the bathroom. And it's right over there." Kevin lifted his arm and pointed to a door with the men's room sign.

"Don't ever do that again," Dan barked.

"Go pee?" he asked, his face scrunching in confusion.

"No! Don't go anywhere without telling me where you're going."

The boy's eyes glistened with tears. "I'm sorry, Uncle Dan. I didn't mean to make you mad."

Dan felt a hodgepodge of emotion he didn't know what to do with: relief that the child was safe, fear that something like this could happen again, embarrassment over his own panicked response in a crowded bakery.

He scooped up Kevin in his arms, determined to hang on to him until he got him safely back to the hotel. Or maybe he just needed to hold him close for some reason he couldn't understand.

Either way, he had his arms full all the way back to the hotel room where he'd left Eva and Kaylee.

Still, his heart continued to pound, and the adrenaline refused to abate.

If anything had happened to Kevin, Dan would have... Hell, he had no idea what he would have done.

When he finally got Kevin back to the door of their hotel room, he put him down on the floor but still held tight to his shoulder. He fumbled for the card that would unlock the door, then let them both into the room.

There was a cartoon on television, and Kaylee, who was dressed for the day in a little pink top, white shorts and sandals, was laughing out loud at the antics of a big, blue bear.

"Breakfast is here," he said. "Where's Eva?"

"She's in the bathroom, getting dressed."

Dan nodded, then set out the food on the table as the kids each took a seat. He cut a ham-and-egg croissant in half, then gave them each a piece.

He could hear the shower going, so it would be a while before Eva came out.

Good, he thought. His heart was still pounding like a son of a gun, and his palms were still damp.

Hell, Kevin had only been missing for about three minutes. But a lot could happen to a kid in a short amount of time. He could have been kidnapped, lost or injured.

When Eva finally came out of the bathroom, looking like a million bucks, he didn't tell her what had happened, how he'd been so intent upon placing his breakfast order that he hadn't even noticed Kevin walking away. How he'd panicked in a public place and lost his cool.

How seeing his nephew again, holding him in his arms, had caused a flood of warmth to fill his chest to the point he could scarcely breathe.

Dan had no idea how he'd admit to that—to anyone. Ever.

But one thing was certain. If he'd had second thoughts about letting Catherine have the twins, he didn't anymore. His moment of neglect, of panic, just proved that he wasn't cut out to be a parent.

He was either going to be the cause of something bad happening, or he'd fall apart after it did.

Still, as he watched the kids giggle, as he spotted the chocolate on Kevin's face, the milk-mustache on Kaylee's upper lip, his heart took an odd, sidelong tumble.

He was going to miss having them around. And it was going to hurt to let them go. But wasn't that the key to love? To parenthood?

A man or woman had to be willing to sacrifice, to let go.

He glanced at Eva, watched her pick at one of the fruit cups he'd brought back to the room.

She'd dressed for the day in a simple yellow dress and sandals. And she'd woven her hair up in some kind of a twist. It looked good like that, although he would have preferred to see it long.

She laughed at something Kaylee said—Dan had been so caught up in his thoughts that he hadn't been paying attention. And then he realized how glad he was that he'd brought her along.

Originally, he hadn't wanted to, but it was nice having reinforcements—especially after the morning he'd had. But he wondered how she'd react when he told her that he planned to give the kids up—if Catherine was willing to take them.

"Are you ready to go?" he asked. "I told Catherine we'd be there around nine."

The kids brightened, and he realized they missed Catherine as much as she'd missed them.

That's good, he told himself. Really good. Yet something slammed into him, something painful and real.

But it was more than just guilt or a sense of responsibility that was hurting. It was…

Well, he didn't know exactly what it was. He supposed it was because he'd gotten attached to Kevin and Kaylee. They were the only family he had left, the only family he'd ever have again.

Losing them meant…

Losing another part of himself. He wasn't sure when it had happened, when he'd grown to care so much about them.

Maybe it was when his sister had brought them to the ranch for the first and only time. Or when he'd heard that Jenny had died, leaving them alone in New York.

Or when he'd left them in Catherine's care after the funeral and had thought he'd choke on the pain and unshed tears all the way back to Texas.

He had no idea when he'd come to have such a personal stake in it all, but he knew one thing: he'd be damned if he'd let anything happen to either Kevin or Kaylee.

Even if that meant handing them over to Catherine for their own good.

Later that morning, they took the subway to Greenwich Village, where Dan's sister had once lived with the twins and Catherine Loza.

Eva had never been in a city larger than Houston before, so she'd never ridden in any form of mass transit other than a bus. In fact, she'd never even imagined doing so in Manhattan, but there was a first for everything, she supposed.

Dan had been incredibly quiet after he returned with breakfast this morning, and she wasn't sure why. She'd tried to draw him out several times to no avail, so she decided to let it go.

Maybe it had something to do with thoughts of his sister's tragic death, with her memory or with grief over her loss. Whatever it was, she decided it didn't concern her.

When they neared the brownstone that had been divided into apartments, Kaylee and Kevin ran ahead, knowing which one was Catherine's.

"Hey, you two!" Dan yelled. "Come back here."

They slowed to a stop, but Dan chased after them, scolding them and insisting they stick close to him.

Eva had been a little uneasy watching them run ahead, too, but she realized it was their old neighborhood, their stomping grounds. They clearly knew where they were going.

Still, she followed closely behind.

Dan, who had each child by the hand, released his grip on Kaylee so he could ring the doorbell.

Eva noticed that he continued to hold Kevin's hand, probably because Kevin tended to act first and think later. Kaylee was quieter, more introspective and nowhere near as impulsive.

As Eva approached the door to Catherine's home, her steps slowed. She wasn't sure why she was here, other than because the kids had invited her. The whole visit had seemed a little...quick and unexpected.

Maybe Dan and Kevin were more alike than she'd thought. More adventuresome and decisive.

When muffled footsteps sounded from inside, Eva couldn't help but wait for the reunion to unfold. She didn't know what she'd been expecting when Catherine answered the door, but certainly not a stunning, stylishly dressed blonde with sea-green eyes, long, curly hair and a vivacious smile. When she spotted the kids, she stooped to give them each a hug.

"Did you miss us?" Kaylee asked.

"More than you'll ever know." Catherine rose to give Dan a warm embrace. "Thanks for bringing them to me."

"I was happy to do it."

Eva continued to stand back, a little uneasy about being here, about taking part in the emotional reunion.

Then Dan turned and drew her into the conversation. "This is Eva, a friend of ours."

There was no use hanging back now, Eva thought, as she moved forward and offered her hand to Catherine in greeting.

"Please, come in." Catherine stepped aside, and the kids immediately entered.

Dan waited for Eva, then followed her in.

The small apartment was decorated in bright colors—red, yellow, blue and a splash of purple here and there. The furniture was black, with chrome and glass accents. The style wasn't one that Eva would have chosen for herself, but it appealed to her in an artsy, contemporary way.

"Can I get you some espresso?" Catherine asked. "Or maybe some fruit juice or herbal tea?"

"Not for me," Dan said. "We just ate."

Eva thanked her for the offer but declined, too.

"Can we see our room?" Kevin asked. "Do you still have our beds?"

"Of course, I do. But I sent most of your toys and books to Texas."

"We know. But we want to see our rooms anyway." Kevin tapped his sister on the shoulder, then both children dashed out of the living room.

"I guess they still think of this as their house," Dan said.

"I'm sure they're adjusting to the ranch."

Dan shrugged. "I'm not sure about that."

Eva wanted to object, to tell him that they were happy in Texas, that Kevin loved having a big yard and a dog who followed him everywhere he went. But she realized that might not be her place.

"I've got a big day planned for us," Catherine told the kids when they returned to the living room. "I called Jimmy and Carly's mom, and we're going to all go to the children's museum. Then we can have lunch at the Riverside Café. You used to love their kids' menu. And after that, we'll play it by ear."

"Cool," Kevin said.

Kaylee turned to Dan and Eva. "You guys will like it, too."

"We're not going with you," Dan said. "We're going to let Catherine have you all to herself. I think you'll have more fun that way."

Eva blinked, a little surprised by the change of events. But she realized Dan was just being nice and allowing Catherine to enjoy the twins without having to share them.

"When are you coming back for us?" Kaylee asked.

"It depends on when you get home. We can come for you this evening—or whenever Catherine calls us."

"Why don't you let them stay the night?" Catherine said. "I've got a big day planned for us. And I've really missed them."

"Sounds good." Dan brightened, his smile crinkling at his eyes. "I'm sure Eva and I will find things to keep us busy."

"In Manhattan?" Catherine laughed. "This city is one big adventure after another. Have fun."

"You, too." Dan gave the lovely blonde another hug, then told the kids to be good, taking time to lift his index finger and point it at Kevin. "And don't you wander away from her."

"I won't, Uncle Dan. Not even if I have to pee really bad."

As Dan and Eva headed for the subway, he didn't say much. In fact, he appeared to be more introspective than before, but she figured it was because he was uneasy about leaving the kids with Catherine. But it seemed as though they were in good hands. And the kids were happy and at ease.

Besides, Catherine was everything Eva wasn't: beautiful, cosmopolitan and artistic by the look of her stylishly decorated apartment with its many paintings on the walls.

A part of her had wanted to find fault with the woman, but when she saw how warm and loving Catherine was with the kids, she couldn't help but like her.

And clearly, the kids loved her.

As they passed a second intersection, Eva broke the silence by saying, "Catherine's nice."

Dan nodded. "She's great with the kids, too."

"You seem sad. Like you miss them already."

"Yeah." He glanced at her, and she saw the weight of emotion in his eyes. "And I hadn't expected it to be so tough."

"It's only for a day and a night," she said. "The time will fly by before you know it."

She expected him to agree or to respond in one way or another. Instead, he seemed to slip deeper into his thoughts.

If she didn't know better, she'd think that he was giving up the kids for good.

Dan and Eva spent the day at the Metropolitan Museum of Art, which turned out to be a whole lot more fun than he'd expected. They had a light lunch, then stopped at a bookstore nearby and picked up some reading material for the trip home.

Before checking out, Eva found the children's section and scanned through quite a few books until she found some for the kids.

She was going to be a great mother, even if she questioned her ability every now and then. Her twins would be lucky to have her. *So would yours,* he thought, then pushed the unbidden idea from his mind.

On the way back to the hotel, they stopped at several shops along the way, just looking and wandering through the aisles. Dan found the city a lot more appealing this time than the last. He supposed it was because he was getting a handle on the place. Or maybe it was nice to have someone with whom he could enjoy it.

"Are you ready to head back to the hotel?" he asked Eva.

"Yes, but..." She glanced around, trying to figure out which way to turn.

He touched her back and pointed her in the right direction, but as they started on their way, he didn't remove his hand for the longest time.

When they finally reached the lobby of their hotel, he took her by the hand and led her to the concierge's desk, where he asked for some restaurant suggestions.

A young man who wore a tag on his jacket that said his name was Alika gave him several options, then added, "If you like Italian food, you'll probably like Carmella's."

"That sounds good to me." Dan turned to Eva. "What do you think?"

"I'm game if you are."

"It's not a bad walk," Alika said. "It's about nine blocks down, and another three or four across."

"Do we need reservations?"

"Probably. If you'd like, I can make them for you."

Dan glanced at his wristwatch. "We'll need at least an hour to freshen up."

"I'll try to get you a table at six o'clock or shortly thereafter."

"Sounds good."

They'd no more than opened their hotel room door when Alika called to confirm their reservations, and an hour later, they were both showered and just about to head out the door.

Eva, who wore a black dress and low slung heels, looked great—and ready for a night on the town.

As she fussed with her hair, Dan was intrigued by her movements, by her facial expressions.

When had he enjoyed watching a woman primp so much? He wasn't sure that he ever had.

As she reached for a clip and began to weave the

strands into a twist of some kind, he said, "Leave it long tonight."

She turned to him, and her lips parted.

Realizing his suggestion had probably sounded as though it had come out of the blue, he added, "Please?"

"You don't want me to wear it up?"

"You've got beautiful hair, Eva." The kind of hair a man liked to let run through his fingers, to see splayed on a pillowcase as he hovered above her.

Oh, for Pete's sake. What was he thinking? But before he could backpedal or tell her that it didn't matter how she fixed her hair, she let the luscious locks fall to her shoulders and set the clip on the table.

Then she smiled, her eyes glimmering like expensive bourbon on ice. "All right, then. I'm ready."

"Great," he said, trying his best to shake it off—the arousal, the romantic images.

It was only dinner, he told himself.

But right this minute, as their gazes met and locked, it seemed like a whole lot more than that. It was a date, a night on the town with a woman he'd been attracted to ever since he'd first laid eyes on her.

And as he opened the door to their room and waited as she stepped out into the hall, leaving a trailing wisp of orange blossoms, he realized that they'd be coming home to the room without any kids to act as a diversion.

He should have been scared spitless, but in all honesty, he couldn't help looking forward to having her all to himself.

Chapter Eleven

They took the elevator down to the lobby, then Dan ushered her through the revolving door that led to the street. He was going to suggest that they walk, since he was finding this trip to New York a little intriguing rather than so intimidating. But Eva was expecting, and he hated to push her to do too much in her condition— not that she appeared to be pregnant tonight.

She was flat-out stunning in that black dress—baby bump or not—and it was nice to have her on his arm.

"It's about a ten- to fifteen-minute walk," he said. "But we can take a cab, if you'd rather."

"Walking is good for me," she said.

All right. Then that was settled.

They set out on a leisurely stroll, window-shopping and people-watching. And he soon found that—unlike on his other trips to New York—the energy of the city, the thrill of being somewhere new, was almost exhilarating.

It wasn't long before they spotted the red awning that Alika had mentioned. Dan pointed ahead. "There it is."

He escorted her into Carmella's, with its hardwood floors, wooden café-style chairs and linen-draped tables.

The host, a young man dressed in black slacks and a white shirt, said, "Good evening" with a slight European accent. "Dinner for two?"

"Yes." Dan placed a hand on Eva's back, felt the gentle curve of her spine.

"Would you like a table inside or out?" the young man asked.

"It doesn't matter to me." Dan, whose hand still rested on Eva's back, asked her preference.

"Outdoors might be nice."

"Very well." The man led them to one of several empty wrought iron tables that had been covered with white linen. A small vase with a single red rosebud sat in the middle of the table, surrounded by several votives.

The host pulled out a chair for Eva, and after she sat, Dan took the seat across from her.

Before leaving them alone, the host handed them hardbound menus. "Your waiter will tell you about the specials this evening."

Dan thanked him, then watched him walk away.

"I'm glad we chose this place," Eva said. "And I don't even care what the food tastes like. The ambience of the restaurant, of this city, is wonderful."

Dan chuckled. "I'm afraid that I do care about the taste. I'm starving."

A busboy brought them water with lemon slices, then placed a basket of warm bread on the table.

Eva rested her forearms on the table, leaned forward and smiled. "It feels a little weird to be having dinner without the kids."

She was right. And it was going to feel a whole lot worse leaving them in New York with Catherine, but he would have to deal with it, knowing that the decision he'd made was for their own good. They had friends here. And the outing Catherine had planned included a trip to the children's museum, for Pete's sake. They certainly couldn't do anything even close to that in Brighton Valley.

Eva reached into the basket and pulled out a slice of crusty bread. "What do you think the kids are doing now?"

"Who knows? But whatever it is, I'm sure they're having fun." And that's exactly what Dan was counting on. He hoped that they'd remember how happy they'd once been in New York. That way, when he sprung the idea of them staying with Catherine, they'd jump at the chance.

And it would sure make it easier on Dan if they did.

The waiter came by and took their orders—two dinner salads with Italian dressing, cheese ravioli for Eva and the lasagna for him.

They made small talk for a while, and as evening descended upon the city and the candles flickered in the votives, they watched the people passing along the sidewalk.

"There's a whole new world out here," Eva said.

"You're right. This isn't anything like Brighton Valley."

"It's a nice change, isn't it?"

He nodded, even though he'd never thought so before he'd brought her, before he'd actually explored the city and had carefully chosen an out-of-the-way restaurant in which to eat.

As she tossed him a pretty smile, he realized that he was glad he'd let the kids talk him into bringing her along. And not just to make the trip easier on him.

She was having a good time; he could see it in her eyes. And now, when she went back to work in the lab, and her coworkers asked how she'd spent her vacation, she could at least tell them she flew to New York for part of the time, that she'd been to the Met, that she'd gone out on the town.

That sure sounded a lot better than telling them that she'd spent the entire two weeks cooking, cleaning and babysitting at a ranch in Brighton Valley.

What a shame it would have been for her to blow her vacation that way.

The waiter served their salads, then quietly slipped away, leaving them to eat.

Dan was hungry, of course. But for some reason, instead of digging in, he took time to watch Eva lift her fork and take the first bite.

"Mmm," she said, clearly savoring the taste. "The dressing is really good."

He really ought to follow suit and reach for his own fork, but he studied her in the candlelight instead, watched the sheen of her hair, the glimmer in her eyes.

She was a beautiful woman, no doubt about that.

And over the past week or so, he'd made up his mind to avoid getting involved with her. But there was no denying a growing attraction on his part.

His biggest worry had been in finding himself trapped in a family-type situation that he couldn't deal with. But with Kaylee and Kevin staying in Manhattan—where they'd be safe and happy—the fear of a romantic involvement with Eva wasn't nearly as strong as it once had been.

And as long as she didn't expect him to take an active role in her babies' lives, he wouldn't mind having a no-strings type sexual relationship with her—if she was willing.

But why would she expect him to be a father to her kids? After all, she'd had in vitro fertilization. Clearly, she hadn't meant to be tied to a man during her pregnancy or afterward.

So he decided to enjoy the night and the woman across from him.

He reached for his fork and tried his best not to wolf down his salad.

Oh, man. Eva had been right. The dressing was out of this world. Or maybe he was just so hungry that anything would have hit the spot about now.

They continued to eat in silence, although every once in a while, he saw Eva glance at the pedestrians walking by, some of whom appeared to be dressed for the theater.

Interestingly enough, the only thing that caught Dan's attention was his dinner date.

And that's just what he considered Eva to be tonight—*his date*. It was funny, he thought. With that realization, even the air he breathed seemed different, the ambience more romantic.

As the waiter removed their empty salad plates, Eva thanked the man, then turned up her scarf.

"If you're getting cold out here," Dan said, "I can ask them to move us to a table inside."

Her movement stilled. "No, I'm fine. Why do you ask? Are *you* cold?"

Should he tell her that he'd seen her fussing with her scarf and that he'd come to the wrong conclusion? Or should he just let it ride?

He'd always been polite and tactful, but in this case? It went deeper than that. And he wasn't so sure that he wanted only a superficial relationship with Eva.

"You don't have to do that," he told her. "Not with me."

Her fingers slowed, and her brow furrowed. "Do what?"

"Try to hide the scar. It's a part of who you are, and it doesn't detract from your beauty in the least."

Her beauty?

Eva's heart strummed at the compliment that had completely caught her off guard.

"You're looking at me as though you don't believe me," he said.

The way he was looking at her, the way he said it, chased away the doubt.

He reached across the table and took her hand in his, removing it from the scarf that draped her neck. Then he pressed his lips against her fingers, his breath warming her from the inside out. "Don't let the past alter the future—or mar your perception of yourself.

You're bright, you're beautiful and you're one hell of a woman, Eva."

Her heart was pounding to beat the band, and tears welled in her eyes. Never had anyone been so sweet, so kind…. Never had an evening been so romantic.

Before she could think of a response, the waiter brought their food. And as he placed the plate of ravioli in front of her, she was no longer hungry. Instead, she was caught up in a heady arousal of sweet words and swirling pheromones.

She was falling deeply, mindlessly in love for the very first time in her life.

Reason insisted that it was too quick, that there was too much for her to consider—his twins, as well as her own. That people didn't really fall in love at first sight—or shortly thereafter.

Instead, it must be the magic of the city, the kindness he'd shown her, the heated gaze that was reaching deep into her heart and turning her inside out.

But for some reason, she couldn't seem to buy a logical explanation now. Not when everything she'd ever wanted but never allowed herself to dream about— a handsome husband who adored her, a happy home, a loving family—seemed to be just a whisper and a heartbeat away.

What was happening to her? She never let emotion get in the way of her judgment, her logic.

Trying to ignore the need to say something warm and mushy that could come back to haunt her later, she picked up her fork and cut into one of the ravioli on her plate.

They were delicious, she decided. But her hunger had taken another turn, one she wasn't prepared for.

What would they do when they got back to the hotel room? Or better yet, what did *she* want to do?

She supposed they'd have to take it one step at a time, but she could see herself kissing Dan again. And she could also see a reason to throw caution to the wind.

But was making love with Dan the right thing to do?

And would he even want to?

She supposed she'd find out soon enough. But as far as she was concerned, the only thing she wanted to do right this minute was to make this night, this feeling that was burning deep within her heart, last forever.

Dan reached into his pocket and pulled out the key card that would unlock the door to their hotel room.

He and Eva had held hands on the way back from the restaurant, which he supposed was a pretty clear sign that their dinner had turned into an actual date. But neither of them talked about the fact that they'd be sharing a hotel room tonight. Nor did they discuss what they'd do once they got back to their room.

Dan certainly had a good idea, though—if Eva was willing.

Now, as he opened the door, he released his hold on her so that she could enter first. As she did, she flipped on the light switch, illuminating the room. Then she slipped the silky scarf from her neck and placed it, along with her purse, on the entryway table.

The room was a lot tidier than it had been when they'd left this morning. There were no reminders of the kids, no toys lying around, no shoes or socks left on the floor.

While they'd been at dinner, the maid had come by

and turned down the beds—both of them. But if he had his wish, they'd only be using one.

As Dan bolted the door for the night, Eva walked to the window and peered through the glass at the city below. Then she slipped off her shoes. Getting comfortable, he supposed.

So now what? Did he turn on the television? Did he plop down on one of the beds and try to make small talk?

He'd never had a difficult time coming on to a woman before, but for some reason, this was different.

Eva was different.

She turned to face him, her cheeks flushed, her hair a little mussed from the breezy night air. "Thanks for a wonderful day, Dan. This trip has been great. I never would have guessed how much fun I'd have. And dinner was wonderful."

"You're welcome." He closed the distance between them, figuring that he'd leave his next move to chance. "Thanks for coming with us and for keeping me company today. I actually enjoyed the city more with you here."

Her smile damn near knocked him off his feet, and something rushed between them. Something that urged him to slip his arms around her waist, to draw her close, to lower his head and place his lips on hers.

As he did, she wrapped her arms around his neck and leaned into him, kissing him right back as though they'd been lovers for as long as either could remember.

He tasted every nook and cranny of her sweet, moist mouth, and his hands slid along the curve of her back, the slope of her derriere. A surge of raging hormones nearly knocked him to his knees. He drew her closer, and as she leaned into him, he gripped her bottom, pulling her against his growing erection.

Could she feel how badly he wanted her?

Apparently so, because she threaded her fingers through his hair, drawing his mouth closer, his tongue deeper. And she arched forward, pressing herself against him.

Had he ever wanted to make love to a woman this badly before? Surely he had, but he couldn't seem to think of any particular woman but this one, any other time but now.

He kissed her harder, deeper, until he thought he'd die if he didn't take her to bed. So he slowly pulled his mouth from hers, his breath ragged. But he didn't let go of her.

"What do you want to do about this?" he asked, hoping she wouldn't suggest that they take things slow and easy. But the ball was in her court.

As Eva tried to recover from the heated kiss that had turned her knees to Jell-O, she thought about Dan's question. What *did* she want to do about it?

There was no use playing games or being coy. They were both adults, and sex was clearly a normal part of life. So she slid him a smile, then placed a hand on his solid, square-cut jaw, felt the light bristle of his after-five shadow. "I suspect we're both wanting to do the same thing." Then she lifted her face and pulled his mouth back to hers.

He nipped at her bottom lip first. The warmth of his breath was still laced with the sweet, creamy taste of the tiramisu they'd shared for dessert, and she feared she'd never get enough of him.

An erotic tingle flooded through her veins, nearly

buckling her knees, and she reached for his shoulder to steady herself. As if completely in tune to her body, to her needs, he tore his mouth from hers long enough to lead her to one of the beds.

She turned her back to him, then lifted her hair so he could unzip her dress. As he did so, he placed a kiss on her shoulder, then slowly peeled the dress away. She shimmied out of it, then let it pool onto the floor.

When she stepped away from the fabric, she turned to face him in her bra and panties.

"Oh, Eva," he said. "You're so beautiful."

Her hand lifted of its own accord, but before she could touch the scar at her throat, he grabbed her wrist.

His gaze seemed to tell her that every inch of her was perfect, unblemished in his eyes.

"It's gone," he told her. "It's not there anymore." Then he pressed a kiss against her throat, his breath warming the ugly spot until it felt…completely healed, normal…beautiful.

She reached behind her and unhooked her bra, freeing her breasts and prepared to offer all she had to him. She was ready to trust him with her body, her heart and her soul.

As Eva's bra dropped to the floor, as she peeled off her panties and stood before him naked, he swallowed—hard.

Her belly formed a definite mound where her babies grew, but for some reason, her pregnancy only made her more beautiful, more desirable.

As she placed her hand on his chest, over the pocket of his shirt, he covered her fingers with his. Could she feel his heart beating like a runaway train?

He unbuckled his belt, then pulled the tails of his shirt from his pants. As she helped him undo the buttons and bare his chest to her, her fingers skimmed across his skin. He shivered at her touch, and heat raced through his blood.

Her breasts were full and round, the dusky pink tips ready for him to touch, to caress, but she stepped forward, embracing him instead and placing skin against skin.

He was lost in a swirl of heat and desire. And all he knew was that he wanted her more than he ever thought possible. He lifted her into his arms, then lay her on the bed.

Moments later, when they were both naked, he joined her between the sheets, loving her with his hands and his mouth until they were both breathless with need.

As he hovered over her, she opened for him, and he entered her. As he thrust deeply, in and out, as her body adjusted to his and she responded to him, they made love as if they'd been meant for each other.

Nothing mattered to Dan other than ensuring that Eva enjoyed every moment of their joining. And by her whimpers, her sweet sighs, he knew that their lovemaking was just as fulfilling for her as it was for him.

Time stood still as they shared an intimacy he'd never known before.

Tonight was one in a million.

And so was Eva.

When they reached a peak and he felt as if he might explode, she cried out with her climax. He shuddered and released along with her, holding her with each ebb and flow. He was afraid to speak, afraid to break whatever spell had been cast on them tonight.

And that's just what it was. Their lovemaking had been magical—for both of them. He'd seen it in her eyes, heard it in her breath, felt it in her arms.

But he didn't dare mention what the day might bring.

When dawn broke over Manhattan, Eva lay in bed with Dan, his arms holding her close, her bottom nestled in his lap. She'd never imagined that sex could be so thrilling, that love could be so…wonderful.

They'd never said the words last night, although she'd been sorely tempted to several different times. Maybe she'd be able to say what was on her heart this morning over breakfast.

She basked in the warmth of his arms, in the gentle rise and fall of his chest. She could have lain there forever if she hadn't needed to use the bathroom.

Hoping not to wake Dan, she carefully pulled free of his embrace. As she did so, he drew her back into his arms and brushed a kiss upon the small of her back. "Where do you think you're going?"

She smiled, and with a voice still sleepy soft, said, "It's time to get up. We've got to go check on the kids. And we've also got a plane to catch this afternoon."

"There's plenty of time to be lazy."

"Yes, I know. But…nature calls."

His grip on her loosened almost reluctantly. "In that case, you'd better go."

She slipped out of bed and went in the bathroom. While she was there, she took a quick shower and brushed her teeth. Then she wrapped and secured a white, fluffy towel around her and returned to the bedroom.

Dan stood near the window, peering into the street.

"The bathroom is all yours," she said.

He turned and smiled, but something appeared to be weighing heavily on his mind.

"What's the matter?" she asked.

"Nothing. Not really. It's just that…" He sighed. "I'm going to ask Catherine to keep the kids."

If he'd thrown a lamp across the room and shattered it against the far wall, he wouldn't have surprised her any more than that.

She felt as though something had been torn right out of her, and she couldn't keep the shock or the confusion from her voice. "Why would you do that?"

"Because it's the right thing to do."

"How do you figure?" she asked, slapping her hands on her hips.

"It's for their own good. Somewhere along the way, I'd fail them. I already have—you know it and so do I."

She eased closer to him, unable to fully grasp what he was saying. "They love you, Dan. You're their uncle."

"Yes, I know. But kids need a mom."

And he thought Catherine would make a better mom than Eva would? Something cracked in her chest, something fragile.

"Kids need someone who loves them," she said. "A man or a woman. It really doesn't matter who. Just someone they can count on, someone who is looking out for them."

"That's what I'm trying to do."

"Are you?"

He didn't respond; he just stood there.

"Do you know what I think?" She crossed her arms and let him have it. "I think maybe you're the one who always wanted and needed a mom."

His eye twitched, as if she'd been on target, so she continued.

"But that doesn't mean you should insist that Kaylee and Kevin have a mother. No one can take the place of the one they had and lost."

He seemed to ponder her words for a beat, then he gave a little shrug. "Okay. Maybe you have a point. Maybe they do love me. Maybe I love them. Maybe I'd do anything to see them happy and healthy. But what can I offer them in Brighton Valley?"

Fresh air came to mind. Wide-open spaces. Dogs and puppies, horses and cattle.

Love. A family.

"I didn't tell you before," Dan said, "but I nearly lost Kevin when I took him to get breakfast yesterday. And it's always been on my watch when one of them got hurt. Can't you see that I'm doing this for them?"

No, she couldn't. And she couldn't help feeling as though whatever he was doing, it was being done to her, as well. Her heart broke at the thought of giving up the kids—and they weren't even hers.

She tried to make sense of it all, but she couldn't seem to understand what Dan was saying.

Was that because she'd grown attached to him and the kids? Was she clinging to the idea of becoming the family that she'd always hoped she would have someday?

And if so, he was dashing her hopes and dreams, too.

"I know how uneasy you feel about taking care of

them," she said, "but I can help out, if you'd like me to. I can take a leave of absence from work...."

"No." The word came out strong, firm. Decisive. Then he softened ever so little and added, "That's not going to help. It's not you. It's me."

Before she could come up with an argument, the phone rang, and Dan answered. "Hello?"

He paused a moment, then said, "Hey, good morning. How's it going?"

Then he grew somber. "We'll be right there."

"What's the matter?" she asked.

"Kaylee was sick all night long, and she's asking for me."

Eva wanted to scream. If Kaylee was sick and asking for Dan, didn't that prove that he'd become more to her than just a legal guardian?

But did that even matter now?

Their gazes locked, and a feeling of remorse settled over her as she watched Dan stride across the room, snatch his pants from the floor and head for the shower.

Something sparked in his eyes, an emotion too elusive for her to decipher.

And it was then that she realized she was in big trouble. She'd fallen in love with a man who refused to be part of a family.

A man who would never love her back.

Chapter Twelve

Dan snatched the pants he'd worn yesterday from the floor and headed for the bathroom. He stopped long enough to shove them into his suitcase, which was on the floor near the closet, and to remove a clean pair of boxers and his favorite jeans.

All he wanted to do was shower, get dressed and check on Kaylee, who was still running a fever this morning.

He also needed to get away from Eva for a little while, to escape the disappointment in her expression.

Didn't she realize he wasn't an ogre? That he would keep the kids with him if he could? That he loved them? That he was only giving them up because he couldn't take care of them in the way they deserved?

I'll help out if you'd like me to, she'd told him just moments ago. *I can take a leave of absence from work.*

But that would only be a temporary solution to his

problem. Once her babies were born, Eva would be a long-term complication, and he'd be a fool to think otherwise. Just seeing her reaction to the decision he'd made about the kids had convinced him of that.

Of course, after what they'd done and all they'd shared last night, it was probably too late to backpedal. He was going to owe her some kind of explanation as to why they couldn't sleep together again, why once would have to be enough.

It was a shame, too. Making love with her had been everything he'd hoped for and more. Even in the morning, when she'd awakened in his arms, he hadn't been uneasy about it. He'd actually lain there, comfortable and content, thinking that they could have an ongoing, no-strings-attached relationship.

But when he'd seen the look on her face after he'd told her he was giving up the kids, he'd realized he'd been mistaken. There would be plenty of strings attached.

In spite of being a scientist and a rational medical professional, Eva wasn't any different from the other marriage-minded women he'd dated over the years. She was clearly a nester. He'd sensed it in her eyes, in the tone of her voice, in her obvious disappointment.

He had to admit that he was feeling something for her, too. He wasn't sure what it was or what it all meant, but it was a lot stronger than he'd expected, and that scared the crap out of him, especially with her babies coming in five short months.

It didn't take a brain surgeon to realize that two sets of twins meant four times the trouble, four times the commitment. It would be an ominous job for even the most experienced of men. And for a guy who wasn't husband or daddy material?

It was out of the question.

When Dan had declined Eva's offer of help, he'd tried to explain that his refusal didn't have anything to do with her. It was all about him and his shortcomings. But the confusion, the pain on her face had unsettled him.

She just didn't get it, and he'd be damned if he knew how to express it any better than he had. So he'd opted for a few minutes alone in the bathroom, where he could wrap his mind around his problem and come up with a solution.

Yet so far, he was drawing a blank.

Now, with the door locked, he turned on the shower. While he waited for the water to heat, he tried to think of what he should have said instead, what he should have done. But he'd be damned if he could come up with anything that wouldn't create some kind of promise he couldn't keep.

What did Dan know about families—or the dynamics that kept them together? Even Jenny, his sister, had abandoned him by making a new life for herself in New York.

So what made him think that he could make a commitment with someone who wasn't even related by blood—or by that special kinship that was supposed to belong to twins?

If Eva knew the half of it, maybe she'd understand how complex and difficult this was for him.

Did she think he was just blowing off his responsibilities? That he would be relieved when he left the kids behind in New York?

Hell, he'd gotten attached to them and would miss them when they were gone. He was going to have to make time to fly out and visit them a couple times a year.

Satisfied with his decision and convinced that the water was hot enough to do the trick, he pulled back the shower curtain and stepped under the steady spray.

Usually, the hot water pounding on his head and shoulders was enough to refresh him, but that wasn't the case today. And escaping Eva hadn't done him any good, either. He still didn't know how to end the relationship they'd started last night.

One way or another, he'd have to do it before she started making plans to become a family.

He'd also have to tell the kids goodbye—and he wasn't looking forward to doing that, either. But he couldn't stay in the bathroom forever, so he shut off the water, reached for a towel and dried himself. Then he dressed and combed his hair. He didn't shave, though. He didn't want to take the time. He had to get to Catherine's to check on Kaylee. Then he'd ask her to keep the kids before he and Eva left for the airport.

When he opened the bathroom door, Eva was packed and ready to go. She'd left her hair down, as though remembering that he liked it that way. And even dressed casually in a pair of sneakers, black denim jeans and a loose-fitting pink T-shirt, she was striking.

But she wasn't smiling.

"Are you ready?" he asked, even though it was clear that she was.

She merely nodded. The fact that she hadn't spoken hadn't gone unnoticed. But what was there to say?

He was leaving the kids with Catherine, unless she refused to take them.

And Eva disapproved of his game plan.

Dan grabbed his suitcase, then took hers, as well. "Okay, let's go."

Minutes later, they'd checked out of the hotel and were headed for the nearest subway station. All the while, their moods were somber, and their words were few.

Using the passes they'd purchased yesterday, they walked through the turnstiles and joined the others waiting for the next car that would take them to Greenwich Village.

Dan stole a glance at Eva, saw that she was deep in thought, that her mood hadn't lifted.

Finally, she said, "I think you're making a big mistake."

"I know you do, and I respect that." But he feared it would be a worse mistake to take the twins home and botch up the whole family thing.

And even if Catherine refused to keep them and he had to take them back to the ranch, it wouldn't solve the problem he now faced with Eva.

She'd already shown her hand. She would want more than a casual sexual relationship—maybe not at first, but it wouldn't take long for that to happen. Look how quickly she'd moved into the house and had taken to the kids. She'd even managed to burrow into his heart, even though he couldn't let her stay there.

He slid another glance her way, saw her brow furrowed.

Maybe he was wrong. Maybe she was realizing that

she'd misjudged him, too. That last night, as wonderful as it had been, had been a mistake.

And if that's what she was thinking, it might make things easier on both of them.

"Listen," he said, "about last night..."

"Don't worry about it. We're both adults. It happened. There's nothing to talk about."

He ought to have been happy to hear her say that, but her words struck an unexpected and raw chord, and they were more unsettling than they should have been.

Eva didn't know what she'd been expecting from Dan any longer. He'd made it perfectly clear that he planned to give up the kids and why it made sense to him.

Kaylee and Kevin were, of course, his kids—not hers. So she wasn't sure why his plan bothered her as much as it did. She felt as though she'd lost something, although she wasn't exactly sure what.

And now, Dan had withdrawn deep within himself, shutting her out, it seemed. And she wasn't sure what to do about that, either—if anything.

Clearly, their lovemaking had only been a physical act to him. A needed release. And the fact that it had meant more to her was tearing her apart.

So was his attitude about the kids.

The closer they got to Catherine's house, the more uneasy Eva got about leaving the twins in New York. But it wasn't because she feared they wouldn't be happy or well cared for. Catherine appeared to be both loving and kind. And the kids clearly liked her.

It's just that Eva thought families should stay together, as long as there weren't any signs of abuse or neglect. But apparently, there was no convincing Dan of that.

Nothing she'd said earlier had made even a small dent in his resolve, and she feared that he'd made up his mind to leave them with Catherine even before he left home on Friday.

So where did that leave her in the mix?

On the outside looking in; that was for sure.

Why had he allowed her to come along with them to New York in the first place? Just to help him with the kids?

Or had he wanted to get her alone? Had he planned to make love with her last night?

She wasn't sure she'd ever learn the answers.

As it was, when the subway car stopped and the doors opened, she stepped inside and held tight to the first pole she came to, bracing herself for the movement.

When they finally reached the stop closest to Catherine's house, they disembarked, pushed through the turnstiles and climbed the stairs to sunlight and fresh air.

Yet Eva still didn't have any clarity in her mind.

They walked several blocks to Catherine's brownstone, entered and knocked on her door.

Moments later, the attractive blonde let them inside. Then she surprised them both by saying, "Kaylee's feeling a little better this morning, but she was asking for both of you last night."

She'd asked for Eva, too? Her heart did a silly little flip-flop at that news.

As she and Dan entered the living room, Eva spotted Kaylee seated on the sofa. Her cheeks were slightly flushed and her eyes were a little dull.

"You're here," she said, first to Dan, then to Eva. "I was really, really sick. And I was afraid I was going to die and go to heaven like Mommy did."

Eva glanced at Catherine, who slowly nodded. Then she made her way to the sofa and took a seat next to the child. "People get sick all the time, sweetheart. But that doesn't mean they're going to die."

Kaylee, whose hair was messy from her rough night, brushed a stray tendril from her forehead. "But I didn't know that. And Catherine didn't know the phone number for the princess doctor."

"I'm sure there are plenty of royal doctors in Manhattan." Eva looked at Catherine and smiled. "She's talking about Dr. Nielson, who works in the E.R. in Brighton Valley."

"Yeah," Kevin said. "But there's only Dr. Carlisle here, and he makes kids get shots, even when they're not sick."

Eva placed a hand over the little girl's brow, trying to gauge her temperature. "How are you feeling now, Kaylee?"

"Better. But I'm glad you and Uncle Dan are here now."

Eva looked at the man who was standing in the center of the floor, still holding their bags.

What had she done? She'd just swept in without thinking, clearly overstepping her boundaries, and her tummy twisted.

Something deep inside of her, an inner voice that urged her to keep to herself, to stay safe and out of the line of fire, urged her to let Dan and Catherine take it from here. Why encourage a relationship that wouldn't amount to anything—and she wasn't just talking about the one with Kevin and Kaylee.

Again she looked at Dan, read the worry and discomfort in his eyes. He really was struggling with the emotional aspects of childrearing, and as angry as she was, as hurt by his attitude, her heart softened toward him just a little.

"Kaylee finally dozed off around three this morning," Catherine said. "And her fever broke. Do you think she should still see a doctor?"

She was asking Eva's opinion?

"I'm not sure," was her answer. E.R. visits could take forever, and some fevers just needed to run their course.

"I suppose you could wait and see how she feels when she gets back to Texas," Catherine said. Then she turned to the kids. "Why don't you go and pack your things? And don't forget the new backpacks and the toys and games I bought you yesterday."

As the kids dashed out of the room, she added, "I thought it might be a good idea for them to have something new to play with while they're flying home."

"Speaking about home," Dan said. "I was wondering if you'd like the kids to live with you, now that your show has ended."

But there would be other shows, Eva wanted to say. And the kids would be left with sitters or daycare workers.

"Sure," Catherine said. "If you'd like me to."

"Stay *here?*" Kevin asked, returning to the room unexpectedly. "In *New York?* But what about Uncle Hank? And Jack and Jill? And what about you, Uncle Dan?"

Great. Dan hadn't expected Kevin to overhear him. And he'd be darned if he wanted the child to get the wrong idea. He'd have to tread lightly here. "You like New York, and you've missed Catherine. Maybe you can come back to Texas during the summer. That way, we can all share you."

"But I'm going to be a cowboy. Remember? And how am I going to learn to ride a horse here?"

"And what about Uncle Hank's birthday cake?" Kaylee asked, returning to the room, as well. "I'm going to help Eva make it."

Dan hadn't expected the kids to put up a fuss—and he wasn't prepared for it.

"I don't mind keeping them," Catherine said. "They really aren't any trouble. But for what it's worth, Kaylee told me numerous times during the night that she just wanted to go home."

Hell, Dan thought. She *was* home.

But he didn't want to argue. And he damn sure wasn't about to look at Eva. He knew how she felt.

But he was drowning here, and he had no idea how to save himself, how to get this runaway conversation back on track. And Eva, who'd come to his aid with maternal wisdom time and again in the past, wasn't going be any help now.

"Don't you want us to be with you all the time?" Kaylee asked.

"It's not that," Dan said. Hell, he didn't want the kids to feel as though he was abandoning them. He knew exactly how that pain felt to a child.

"We do like it here," Kevin said. "But we like living with you better."

The pure innocence in the child's face, the honesty

in his words, reached deep inside of Dan, softening his heart, crushing his resolve.

So he took a deep breath, then slowly let it out and said, "Okay. Then I guess we're all going back to Brighton Valley."

The decision had been made, and he'd stick with it. But what in the hell was he going to do about Eva?

After Eva helped secure the kids in their car seats, she climbed into the passenger side of Dan's pickup and shut the door.

The flight to Houston had been fairly routine. Dan had asked Kevin to empty his pockets before going through the metal detector. He was learning from his mistakes and planning ahead.

Kaylee wasn't complaining, but she wasn't her usual self. And since Eva and Dan were still tiptoeing around the words they'd had earlier and dealing with the pall that had fallen upon their short-lived relationship, Kevin did most of the talking from Houston International to Brighton Valley.

But as they neared the ranch, Kaylee finally chimed in. "How much longer before we get to the ranch?"

"Just a few more minutes," Dan told her.

When Kaylee had been sick in New York, all she'd wanted to do was to go home. Had Dan finally realized that the "home" she'd been talking about was the one in which she lived with him?

Eva wanted to tell him that and to encourage him to trust in his ability to parent the children, but she feared that it wasn't in her best interest to open herself up for more rejection.

She couldn't very well embrace the children who

desperately needed a mommy and the rancher who needed a loving wife more than he'd ever admit. If she did, she would risk getting her heart broken in the process. Besides, she would soon have a family of her own to think about.

When they got back to the ranch, she would pack her clothes and head home. She needed to make a break from Dan and the twins before she grew too close to a family that would never be hers.

They arrived as dusk settled over Brighton Valley. But rather than leave immediately, she would fix the kids something to eat. And while she was tucking them into bed, she'd explain to them why she wouldn't be there when they woke up in the morning.

Of course, she wasn't sure what reason she'd give them. She could hardly understand it herself.

While Dan unloaded the suitcases from the back of the pickup, she followed the kids into the house.

Hank met them at the door, clearly glad to see them home.

If the crotchety old man had been softened by the children, Eva had a feeling Dan would soon be right behind him.

"How was your trip?" Hank asked.

"It was fine," Eva said.

"Did you eat dinner yet?" he asked.

"No. I thought I'd make something light and easy, like canned soup and grilled-cheese sandwiches. Is that okay with you?"

Dan, who'd just entered the house with both bags, said, "Sounds good to me."

He took her bag to her room, then carried his upstairs. And while the kids told Hank about their trip to the children's museum, Eva slipped into the kitchen and made them a bite to eat.

As soon as she'd announced that everything was ready, Kaylee was the first to enter, so Eva took time to feel her forehead, to check to see if she was still warm.

And she was.

Maybe a call to Betsy Nielson was in order. If the fever was a sign of something serious, they might need to take Kaylee to the E.R. And if it wasn't anything to be worried about, then maybe Eva—or rather Dan—could call the pediatrician in the morning and make an appointment.

So while the men and children took a seat at the table, she excused herself and went into the living room to place the call to the E.R., where she expected to find the dedicated doctor who'd become a good friend.

It took several minutes for Betsy to get to the telephone, and once she was on the line, Eva explained the situation. "I don't have a thermometer, but she's still warm to the touch."

"Is she complaining of any pain?"

"No. Last night, she had a tummy ache, but that seems to be better today."

"I think you can wait until tomorrow. If her temperature spikes later, you might want to bring her in. Do you have any fever reducer?"

"I don't think so, but I'm not sure."

"Then you probably should go to the drugstore and pick up a thermometer and some children's Motrin to have on hand."

"Will do," Eva said, thinking she'd pass the word on to Dan. The sooner she got out of here, the better.

Yet just the thought of leaving was breaking her heart, but she had no other choice. She might have fallen in love with Dan, but there was no future for them.

She heard a noise in the background, a nurse talking, a radio squawking.

"What's going on?" she asked.

"Just the usual."

Someone interrupted Betsy again, and Eva decided to hang up, but she'd wait until she had the doctor's attention.

Betsy sighed into the receiver. "Dawn just notified me that we've got an ambulance en route with a man who was beaten and robbed. He's unconscious and with no wallet or ID on him. We have no way of knowing who he is or anything about his medical history, so we'll have go by trial and error. His ETA is about three minutes, so I need to go."

"Thanks, Betsy. Have a good evening."

"You, too."

Yeah, right. Eva ended the call, then headed back to the kitchen, passing the twins on her way.

"Where are you going?" she asked.

"We're done eating, and Uncle Dan told us to turn on the bath water, then wait for him. He's going to come upstairs in a minute and help us."

Apparently Dan was planning to oversee the bath time himself, which was proof that he was taking his job seriously.

And that he was cutting Eva out.

Tears welled in her eyes, and an ache settled deep in her heart. She'd come to love Dan and the kids. She wanted nothing more than to be a part of this family, to make them all a part of hers.

But that wasn't going to happen. She and Dan had only been playing house. And now that he was becoming the parent the children needed, it was time for her to go.

As she drew close to the kitchen, she heard Dan talking to Hank.

"We need a nanny in the worst way, and I don't know what else to do about it. I've had an ad in the paper for a week now, and I haven't had a single call."

So Eva wasn't the only one who realized that she and Dan couldn't continue to play house forever. Still, the truth hurt, especially coming from him. She was just about to continue into the living room when Hank asked. "What about Eva?"

"She's got to go back to work," Dan said. "And I'm getting desperate. You'd think that someone would have answered that ad."

"Actually," Hank said, "you've had quite a few calls."

There was a beat of silence, then Dan responded, his tone sharp. "Why didn't you tell me?"

"I didn't see a need to. And I told each one of them that the position had been filled."

"Why in the hell did you do *that?*"

"Because I like Eva. And I think you ought to do whatever it takes to make her stay."

Eva's heart warmed at the elderly man's words, and even though she felt like a snoop, she waited to hear Dan's response.

But Hank was the one who spoke next. "You ought

to marry her, Dan. You need a woman, and so do the kids."

"The kids might need a mom," Dan told his uncle. "But I don't need anyone."

Eva's stomach clenched. As much as she'd love to create a family with Dan and the twins—both hers and his—she wanted more than a father for her babies. She wanted a man who loved her. And not just any man; she wanted Dan.

But she wouldn't settle for less than she deserved, less than she wanted, even if that meant packing up and going back to her place.

So she entered the kitchen as if she hadn't heard a word they'd said and announced she was leaving.

"Tonight?" Dan said. "You haven't eaten yet."

"I'm really not hungry."

"What about the kids?" he asked.

"You're doing great with them. You don't need me."

At the near repetition of what he'd just said to Hank, Dan's gut clenched. Had she overheard them talking?

When Hank had said he needed a wife, the thought had crossed his mind, but he struggled with loving or needing anyone. He'd been hurt and disappointed by people too often in the past.

"Why not spend the night?" Dan suggested. "There's no need for you to drive home in the dark."

"No, I really think it's best if I leave."

"Well, before you do, I think we need to talk."

She gave a little shrug, as though she couldn't care less, but he knew better. And a wave of guilt settled over him for not having that conversation sooner.

A part of him wondered if he was dragging his feet for a reason, if he actually wasn't as eager to end things between them as he'd once thought.

So he followed her into the guestroom in which she'd been staying and watched as she packed her things.

Instead of feeling a sense of relief, fear rose in his chest. And not just at being left to handle the kids on his own.

He was losing her, and he had no one to blame but himself. "I…uh…I've been a jerk today."

She merely looked at him, but she didn't argue, which only made him feel worse.

"Last night was incredible. But I'm scared."

"Of what?"

"Of parenting the kids. Of being a father to yours…"

"I assumed as much." She opened the closet and began to pull her clothes from the hangers, but she didn't take time to fold them.

Damn. She was in a big hurry to escape, and he really couldn't blame her. She'd stepped in and been a helpmate to him—with no strings attached. And what had he done for her in return?

"I'm sorry, Eva. I really care for you." Care? It went deeper than that, and he knew it. But did he risk admitting it?

Or was the bigger risk in keeping it to himself?

"I might even be in…"

Her movements stopped, and she looked at him— *really looked*. She expected him to finish what he'd started, and while he wanted to, he was as afraid of being honest as he was in lying.

"I'm scared," he admitted. "Okay?"

"Scared of what?"

She wasn't making this easy for him, but then, he supposed he didn't deserve to be treated with kid gloves. But a rising sense of panic was filling him up at the thought of her leaving, and not because of the kids.

It was Dan who'd be hurting, who'd be losing out, if she left. Because he realized he would be a better dad, a better man, a better everything with Eva at his side.

And it didn't matter how many kids they had between them.

"I'm scared of failing, of not being the kind of husband or father a family needs. Everyone I ever loved deserted me one way or another. My mom, my dad. Even my sister."

"You mean, by her death?" Eva asked.

"Yes, but even before that. I wasn't ready for her to move away in the first place. I needed her in my corner, and I got angry when she wanted more out of life—more than a brother with a cowboy heart could give her."

"Jenny didn't leave you, Dan. She had a dream, a big one and she couldn't find in Brighton Valley. And she left to pursue it."

"I realize that now. But my resentment cheated us out of a close relationship for almost twenty years. And now that she's gone—really gone—I can't apologize or do anything about making things right."

They said that confession was good for the soul, and maybe they were right, because the weight of his guilt, as heavy as it was, began to lift ever so slightly, just by opening up his heart and sharing it all with Eva.

"Jenny loved you, Dan. And she respected you.

That's why she made you the guardian of her children. She knew you'd do right by them."

"But what if she was wrong?" He raked a hand through his hair. "Don't you see, Eva? I love you. And I might want a family more than anything in the world, but I don't know how to be a part of one."

Her gaze, as warm and smooth and soothing as brandy, locked on his. "I don't have a good family experience, either. And I'm afraid, too. But I love you, and I know we can work through this."

Somehow, he wanted to believe her.

Aw, hell. He had no other choice but to believe her. Life without Eva was no longer a viable option.

He stepped closer and narrowed the gap between them, which was easy to do in the tiny bedroom. "Say it again."

"That I love you?"

He nodded, wondering why the burden he'd been carrying no longer weighed him down. "And tell me again that we can make this work."

When she smiled, his heart tumbled end over end.

"I love you," she said. "And while I can't assure you that the kids won't get hurt or sick along the way, there's something I *can* promise. No matter what happens, I won't ever leave you. I'm in it for the duration—if you are."

His heart just about blasted out of his chest as he wrapped her in his arms and held her close. "You've got yourself a deal."

Then he kissed her with all the love in his heart. He had no idea what the future would bring, but they'd face it together.

As he drew her closer, as their tongues mated, a

shriek sounded upstairs, followed by a couple of thuds.

"Oh, for Pete's sake," Dan said, ending the all-too-brief kiss. "Now what?"

"Uncle Dan!" Kaylee shrieked again. "Come quick!"

He rushed out of the room with Eva on his heels.

The child yelled again. "The bathtub is running over on the floor!"

By this time, Hank had entered the living room. "Who's watching them up there?"

"It's my fault," Dan said, taking the steps two at a time. "I told them to fill the tub, then forgot all about it."

"That ain't like you," Hank said.

"I was kissing Eva, and I guess I just lost my head." He'd lost his heart, too. But none of that mattered.

And neither did the water on the floor.

When Dan and Eva reached the bathroom, Kevin met them at the doorway. "You told us to turn the water on, but you didn't tell us to stay in here and watch it. You said you'd be up in a minute."

"Yeah," Kaylee chimed in. "And it was a really long minute."

"Well, I guess I messed up," Dan said, as he shut off the faucet and pulled the drain. "But from what I understand, all parents make mistakes now and then."

"That's okay," Kevin said. "want me to help you clean it up?"

"Thanks, sport. I'd appreciate that." Dan glanced at Eva and smiled. "Since I have help, maybe you can go and unpack your things. Or, better yet, why don't we bring them up to my room?"

A smile burst across her face. "That sounds like a plan to me."

"You mean, Eva's going to stay with us?" Kevin asked. "Here on the ranch?"

"Would you like that?" Eva asked.

Kaylee clapped her hands. "I'd *love* it."

"Awesome," Kevin said, grinning from ear to ear. "We can pretend you're our mom."

"You won't need to pretend," Dan said, as he grabbed a towel from the linen closet, then winked at Eva. "She's in this for the duration."

"What's *that* mean?" Kevin asked.

"It means *forever*," Eva said. Then she took Kaylee by the hand and walked her downstairs.

Dan's heart swelled in spite of the mess he was going to have to clean up. And while heaven only knew what might be in store for them over the years, he and Eva would weather the storms together.

When the floor had been mopped up and the wet towels were going through the wash cycle, Dan returned to the living room, where Eva was talking to Hank.

"On the bright side," he said, "the bathroom floor is as clean as a whistle."

Eva slipped up beside him and wrapped her arms around his waist. "Being a family is going to be an adventure for us, Dan, and we'll just have to take one day at a time."

She was right, Dan realized. And they'd be taking one night at a time, too—starting with this one, as soon as the house was quiet.

He turned and brushed his lips across hers, teasing them both with what was to come.

One day, one night, one kiss at a time.

Epilogue

After returning from a cattle auction in Wexler, Dan entered the service porch, removed his hat and jacket and hung them up on the hooks by the back door. The mouthwatering aroma of dinner cooking in the Crock-Pot hit him head-on, and he was reminded that he'd skipped lunch.

Eva was a great cook, and he wondered what she was making—something tasty, no doubt. But before taking a peek inside the pot, he would look for his family.

His family.

It was amazing. Life on the ranch had certainly turned out to be a lot different from what he'd once thought it would be, but Dan couldn't be happier.

Four months ago, on a sunny autumn afternoon, he and Eva had gotten married in a small ceremony at the Brighton Valley Community Church, where they'd promised to love each other for the rest of their lives—a vow they intended to keep.

Kaylee and Kevin had been thrilled to have a "real family" again.

One of Eva's coworkers, a mother of two grown children, had stayed on the ranch and looked after Hank and the twins so the newlyweds could spend a three-day honeymoon in San Antonio.

Eva had taken a leave of absence from the medical center, telling her boss that she'd come back to work when the youngest twins were in school. For now, she wanted nothing more than to be a wife and mother.

And what a great wife and mom she'd turned out to be.

"Hey," Dan called from the kitchen. "Where is everyone?"

"We're in here," Kevin responded, "taking care of the babies."

Dan smiled as he made his way to the living room.

Kevin and Kaylee, who'd celebrated their sixth birthdays in October, were excelling in first grade at Sam Houston Elementary. They were also making friends and socializing, something Eva insisted was important. Still, they seemed happy to be at home and helping with the newest members of the family.

After Eva's second ultrasound last September, she and Dan had known they were having baby girls and had planned accordingly. But nothing had prepared Dan for the rush of love he'd felt the moment Dr. Shaw had placed the first tiny bundle in his arms.

Oh, sure. There were still moments when he worried

that he'd do something wrong, that he'd be too rough
with little Emily or Christy, but there were many more
moments of absolute awe and joy. Eva insisted that
all new daddies felt that way, and she was probably
right.

As Dan entered the living room, Kaylee was watching Eva wrap Emily in a pink flannel receiving blanket.
And Kevin stood by the rocker, where Hank held a
sleeping Christy.

It was easy to tell the newborns apart, since Christy
had more hair. But other than that? They were both as
pretty as their mommy.

"How's everyone doing?" he asked.

Eva brightened when she saw him, clearly glad he
was home. And again he was reminded just how very
much he loved her, how happy they were.

"We're doing just fine," Eva said, as she carefully
placed little Emily in Kaylee's open arms. Then she
met Dan in the center of the room for a welcome-home
hug.

He brushed his lips across hers, then allowed the
kiss to linger a moment. When it ended, Eva remained
in his arms, as they savored their embrace.

It was nice to be home, Dan decided. And in spite of
the chaos that sometimes broke out—the spilled milk,
the occasional squabbles between siblings, the stubbed
toes and skinned knees—he couldn't imagine being
anywhere else when the sun went down.

"Look," Kaylee said, as she studied the seven-pound
newborn in her arms. "Emily's smiling at me."

Dan figured it was just gas, which is what Eva
had told him when he'd coaxed a similar smile out

of Christy yesterday. But he wasn't about to rain on Kaylee's parade.

"That's a definite smile," he said. "She sure loves her big sister."

"She loves *me,* too," Kevin chimed in.

"Yep, she sure does." Dan couldn't help but chuckle as he remembered the day Kevin had first learned that Eva was having two girls, rather than boys or one of each.

He'd been disappointed at first, but Dan had taken him aside and said, "You and I are going to have our hands full, protecting our girls."

The boy had given it some thought, then slowly nodded. "Yeah. That's because we're cowboys. And cowboys always protect little babies, girls and ladies."

"You've got that right," Dan had said. "And if we do our part, the girls and ladies will look after us, too."

Kevin had slipped his hand into Dan's, giving it a boy-size squeeze that warmed a man-size heart.

He was going to enjoy showing Kevin how to be a cowboy, as well as how to be a man.

Of course, Kaylee and the little girls would be welcome to ride the range, too—if that's what they wanted to do. But these days, Kaylee was talking about being a "royal doctor," just like Betsy Nielson.

"Are you ready for dinner?" Eva asked, as she stepped out of their embrace and reached for Dan's hand. "We're having a chicken casserole."

"Sounds good to me." In fact, just about everything Eva suggested sounded pretty good to Dan these days.

He supposed love and family did that to a man.

As they walked together to the kitchen, he couldn't help thinking that his and Eva's lives had the makings of a real-life fairy tale.

Especially the happy ever after.

* * * * *

*Don't miss the next book in Judy Duarte's
new miniseries,*
BRIGHTON VALLEY MEDICAL CENTER
*On sale November 2010,
wherever Silhouette Books are sold.*

COMING NEXT MONTH

Available August 31, 2010

SPECIAL EDITION

REQUEST YOUR FREE BOOKS!

2 FREE NOVELS PLUS 2 FREE GIFTS!

SPECIAL EDITION
Life, Love and Family!

YES! Please send me 2 FREE Silhouette® Special Edition® novels and my 2 FREE gifts (gifts are worth about $10). After receiving them, if I don't wish to receive any more books, I can return the shipping statement marked "cancel." If I don't cancel, I will receive 6 brand-new novels every month and be billed just $4.24 per book in the U.S. or $4.99 per book in Canada. That's a saving of 15% off the cover price! It's quite a bargain! Shipping and handling is just 50¢ per book.* I understand that accepting the 2 free books and gifts places me under no obligation to buy anything. I can always return a shipment and cancel at any time. Even if I never buy another book from Silhouette, the two free books and gifts are mine to keep forever.

235/335 SDN E5RG

Name   (PLEASE PRINT)

Address   Apt. #

City   State/Prov.   Zip/Postal Code

Signature (if under 18, a parent or guardian must sign)

Mail to the Silhouette Reader Service:
IN U.S.A.: P.O. Box 1867, Buffalo, NY 14240-1867
IN CANADA: P.O. Box 609, Fort Erie, Ontario L2A 5X3

Not valid for current subscribers to Silhouette Special Edition books.

Want to try two free books from another line?
Call 1-800-873-8635 or visit www.morefreebooks.com.

* Terms and prices subject to change without notice. Prices do not include applicable taxes. N.Y. residents add applicable sales tax. Canadian residents will be charged applicable provincial taxes and GST. Offer not valid in Quebec. This offer is limited to one order per household. All orders subject to approval. Credit or debit balances in a customer's account(s) may be offset by any other outstanding balance owed by or to the customer. Please allow 4 to 6 weeks for delivery. Offer available while quantities last.

Your Privacy: Silhouette is committed to protecting your privacy. Our Privacy Policy is available online at www.eHarlequin.com or upon request from the Reader Service. From time to time we make our lists of customers available to reputable third parties who may have a product or service of interest to you. If you would prefer we not share your name and address, please check here. ☐

Help us get it right—We strive for accurate, respectful and relevant communications. To clarify or modify your communication preferences, visit us at www.ReaderService.com/consumerschoice.

SSE10R

HARLEQUIN®

A *Romance*

FOR EVERY MOOD™

Spotlight on
Heart & Home

Heartwarming romances
where love can happen
right when you least expect it.

See the next page to enjoy a sneak peek
from Harlequin Superromance®,
a Heart and Home series.

Police chief Juliette Tremblant recognized the shape of the man strolling down the street—in as calm and leisurely fashion as if it were the middle of the day rather than midnight. She slowed her car, convinced her eyes were playing tricks on her. It had been a long time since Tyler O'Neill had been seen in this town.

As she pulled to a stop at the curb, he turned toward her, and her heart about stopped.

"What the hell are you doing here, Tyler?"

"Well, if it isn't Juliette Tremblant." He made his way over to her, then leaned down so he could look her in the eye. He was close enough to touch.

Juliette was not, repeat, *not* going to touch Tyler O'Neill. Not with her fingers. Not with a ten-foot pole. There would be no touching. Which was too bad, since it was the only way she was ever going to convince herself the man standing in front of her—as rumpled and heart-stoppingly handsome now as he'd been at sixteen—was real.

And not a figment of all her furious revenge dreams.

"What are you doing back in Bonne Terre?" she asked.

"The manor is sitting empty," Tyler said and shrugged, as though his arriving out of the blue after ten years was casual. "Seems like someone should be watching over the family home."

"You?" She laughed at the very notion of him being here for any unselfish reason. "Please."

He stared at her for a second, then smiled. Her heart fluttered against her chest—a small mechanical bird powered by that smile.

"You're right." But that cryptic comment was all he offered.

Juliette bit her lip against the other questions.

Why did you go?

Why didn't you write? Call?

What did I do?

But what would be the point? Ten years of silence were all the answer she really needed.

She had sworn off feeling anything for this man long ago. Yet one look at him and all the old hurt and rage resurfaced as though they'd been waiting for the chance. That made her mad.

She put the car in gear, determined not to waste another minute thinking about Tyler O'Neill. "Have a good night, Tyler," she said, liking all the cool "go screw yourself" she managed to fit into those words.

It seems Juliette has an old score to settle with Tyler.
Pick up TYLER O'NEILL'S REDEMPTION
to see how he makes it up to her.
Available September 2010,
only from Harlequin Superromance.

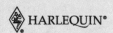

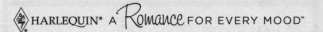